# Agnes Rossi

is the author of one p₁ᵣ
which won the New York Universi₁,
1987. She lives in New York City.

'Ms Rossi tells her story in an unadorned, economical style, a style in which the clarity of common sense becomes a kind of wisdom. This does not, however, prevent her from braiding the past and present into a lovely design that gives *The Quick* its haunting complexity.'
*New York Times Book Review*

'The charm of Rossi's fiction lies in its tender affirmations and disinclination to affix blame. She is insightful, delicate, sometimes funny, and in sure control. A genuine and welcome talent.'
*Kirkus Reviews*

'*The Quick* is an almost flawless study in sensibility. Five months after her father's death, Marie Russo lets her mind range over her past, starting with her first real experience of death and grief. Spinning out from this central event, Marie's relationships with parents, brother, college boyfriend, husband and daughter are poignantly revealed. Using unadorned but forceful prose, Agnes Rossi's unblinkingly observed stories exact the reader's full response, meting out reward in kind.'
*Publishers Weekly*

'If *The Quick* were a speech, it would be interrupted from time to time with applause. It is a privilege to read such fine work by a young writer at the beginning of what will surely be a distinguished career.'
MARY WARD BROWN

AGNES ROSSI

# The Quick

Flamingo

*An Imprint of* HarperCollins*Publishers*

| *f l a m i n g o* | The term 'Original' signifies publication direct into paperback with no preceding British hardback edition. |
| **O R I G I N A L** | The Flamingo Original series publishes fine writing at an affordable price at the point of first publication. |

Flamingo
An Imprint of HarperCollins*Publishers*,
77–85 Fulham Palace Road,
Hammersmith, London W6 8JB

First published in Great Britain by Flamingo 1992
Published by arrangement with W.W. Norton & Company, Inc., US

9 8 7 6 5 4 3 2 1

'The Quick', 'Hungry Dog', 'What You Leave Out', 'The Size of a House',
'Diamonds', 'Scrawl', 'Morpheus' © Agnes Rossi 1992
'Athletes and Artists', 'Teeth and Nails' and 'Breakfast, Lunch, and
Dinner'© New York University 1987

The Author asserts the moral right to
be identified as the author of this work

Author photograph by Fredric Petters

A catalogue record for this book is
available from the British Library

ISBN 0 00 654496 7

Set in Goudy Old Style

Printed in Great Britain by
HarperCollinsManufacturing Glasgow

For Henry Hook

# Contents

The Quick
9

Hungry Dog
89

What You Leave Out
99

The Size of a House
109

Diamonds
121

Athletes and Artists
129

Teeth and Nails
143

Breakfast, Lunch, and Dinner
155

Scrawl
167

Morpheus
179

# Acknowledgments

I'D LIKE to thank my friend and editor Dan Conaway for his honesty and hard work and the New Jersey State Council on the Arts for its support.                    —A.R.

# The Quick

THIS is a neighborhood of people who aren't quite making it. The man next door keeps chickens. Across the street is a house with a supermarket-style door, glass and stainless steel. The stairs up to my apartment used to be part of a ship. They're metal grids, hell on high heels, treacherous after a freezing rain. From down below, from the apartment of my landlord, an enterprising young man who feels betrayed by the decline in real estate values, comes the most awful grinding noise. Our mailman is moody, told me to go fuck myself once, makes his deliveries in a dark green Chevette.

Tonight I was in bed by ten, up at midnight, dragged my bedspread outside so I could sit on the stairs, drink a little bourbon, listen to the night sounds of my neighbor's birds. I learned long ago to take trouble outside. There is something accommodating about the peculiar stillness of a suburban street after midnight. Phyllis and I used to sit on her steps until two or three in the morning. Her voice, loosened by gin, would sound exactly right amidst parked cars, silent streets, dark houses.

I close my eyes and can see Phyllis sitting at her desk in the office we shared at Meyer Brothers, a department store in Paterson, New Jersey. We were responsible for charge accounts and installment purchases. It seems quaint to me now, Phyllis and I in that windowless room with our adding machines and carbon paper. Today I mail my credit card payments to P.O. boxes in the Southwest. My statements all have that strip of computer hieroglyphics across the bottom. In 1962 you sent your check right to the store.

To get to our office, you had to take the elevator to the fourth floor then walk down a short staircase. Our isolation was such that we didn't even get in-person mail delivery. A chute ran from the mail room to us. I remember the creak of the metal door and the gentle thud of paper.

Phyllis was thirty-four; I was twenty-two. She was tall and skinny, too skinny she thought, so she used to drink a high-calorie liquid called Wate-On. I can still see the label so clearly: a smiling, sturdy-looking girl in a two-piece bathing suit leaping in the air to smack a beach ball. At ten and again at two, Phyllis would drink a bottle of Wate-On and eat a couple of teaspoons of peanut butter from the jar she kept in her desk. She acted like it was medicine, staring solemnly into space while she licked the spoon.

If a human being can have a physical opposite, Saul, our boss, was Phyllis's. He was five-two, paunchy, olive-skinned. She dressed conservatively, A-line skirts, cotton blouses. He had a green suit and several ties with animals on them. Her white-blond hair started each day in a modest bouffant but was flat and wispy by lunchtime. His hair was thick, curly, blue-black. In dreamier moments I'd think of us as points on a spectrum. On one end Phyllis, spare and straight as a picket fence, on the other swarthy, bug-eyed, maroon-pants Saul, and in the middle me. I could have been their daughter.

Phyllis's husband died of a heart attack at thirty-eight. She and I were at our desks when the call came. She answered the phone and her voice skidded from crisp efficiency to shock and fear. "Billing, Phyllis Macdonald speaking . . . oh my God . . . my God." One minute we were safe, even bored, opening mail, stamping checks, and the next Phyllis was looking at me wild-eyed, telling me her husband was on his way to St. Joseph's Hospital in an ambulance. She grabbed her purse then shuddered hard.

Saul stuck his head in the door just then.

"Something's the matter with Jim," I said. "She has to go to the hospital."

He stepped out of the way and pointed to me. "You go with her."

I hesitated, wishing all three of us could go. Phyllis passed in front of Saul and I had to run to catch up with her.

There were still cabs in downtown Paterson then. Phyllis stood in the street waving her arms and saying come on, come on. She twitched and shrugged like a kid about to throw a tantrum. I saw the 74 bus heading our way. It would, I knew, take us right down Main Street to the hospital. I told Phyllis we should get on it and she nodded, looking ready to do whatever I said.

As I dropped our fare in the box, Phyllis leaned toward the driver who looked impatient and surly. "My husband's just had a heart attack," she said. "I have to get to St. Joseph's. Please, no cabs would stop."

The driver's expression, his whole demeanor, softened. He looked at Phyllis for a couple of seconds then sat up straight, motioned for us to step behind the line, grabbed the wheel with both hands, took off. We careened past Woolworth's, past the cathedral, pushed through yellow lights, let nobody on or off. The bus rattled so loudly I thought it might simply come apart, leave pieces of itself in its wake.

It was a magnificent display and it gave me hope. Screaming down Main Street on the 74 with the other passengers, mostly old ladies—women, it occurs to me now, whose husbands were most likely dead—telling each other what was going on and being game, seemed action enough to stop anything.

The emergency room was quiet, the waiting area nearly empty. At the desk Phyllis said, "My husband . . ." and was waved through a turnstile. I sat down to wait. All of the urgency of getting to the hospital was over and there I was, breathing hard. I decided I should pray, put my hand over my eyes. Please let Jim be all right. Pretty soon I was just saying please, please, please.

I heard a sucking sound and opened my eyes. A boy and a girl sat in the corner kissing feverishly, necking I'd have called it then. The girl wore a gym suit, a royal blue garment with elastic at the thighs and snaps down the front. I'd had one just like it. I wondered what had happened in gym class and how these two had managed to parlay it into a date of sorts. The girl, opening her eyes for the first time since I'd come in, looked right at me, blinked a couple of times, went back to kissing with renewed vigor. God help Phyllis, I thought guiltily.

A nurse motioned for me from the desk. She leaned forward and spoke softly but distinctly. "Are you Mrs. Macdonald's sister?"

"No, we work together. I came with her."

She nodded. "The news is very bad, I'm afraid." She guided me through the turnstile—I closed my eyes and went—then put her arm on my shoulder and turned me so that our backs were toward the waiting area. "Mr. Macdonald passed away in the ambulance. I'm very sorry."

Her nametag said Mrs. Scanlon, no first name. She had a kind face, droopy eyes, no makeup. I could only think to ask where Phyllis was.

"With him still. I'm going to take you to where you can wait for her."

Mrs. Scanlon had taken two or three steps before I was able to move. I wanted to go back to the lobby, call my parents or Saul. I had no idea what was expected of me in Phyllis's presence.

We walked past sinks and canvas screens on wheels, Mrs. Scanlon a few steps ahead. My eyes lit on her rounded shoulders and stayed there. Even then I kept a narrow focus in hospitals. She waited for me at the entrance to a corridor and from there we walked side by side.

She took me to a small room. There were framed photographs on the walls, blowups of flowers with beads of dew on them. The air smelled as if thousands of cigarettes had been smoked there. "Have a seat," she said gently. "I'll bring Mrs. Macdonald in when she's ready."

I was alone then and reluctant to step out of the doorway. The room seemed like somewhere I shouldn't be, like a morgue or the place in a funeral home where they wash and dress bodies. After a few minutes I sat on the couch as if taking my place there was worth something.

Phyllis was with Jim still, the nurse had said. I imagined her standing beside a stretcher, head down, crying. I couldn't, though, imagine Jim dead. How could it be that here in this place where I was sitting on this couch, somewhere in one of its rooms, Jim who always looked right in my eyes when he talked to me was dead? I wanted to see it, see him, and was ashamed.

I used to wonder how Phyllis had won Jim's love so completely. She wasn't homely, just plain, sober-looking, not at all the sort of woman I'd come to understand men like Jim fell for. He was handsome by anybody's definition. Lively blue eyes, rectangular forehead, strong chin. He had a kind of limber masculinity. To me he was the genuine article. I'd been surprised when I first met him, expected a neutral male presence, someone bland like Phyllis, but turned instead to find blue-eyed Jim who smiled and said, "Pleasure."

At that point I'd been to only one wake, my uncle's father who I couldn't remember ever seeing alive. No one took me up to the casket—women ran a kind of interference, keeping children back—but when it came time for everyone to say a prayer, I pushed my way to the front, determined to get a good look at the corpse. I stared hard at the old man's face until my mother pulled me away by the bow on the back of my dress. Later I played tag among the hearses in the parking lot but there was a ringing in my ears as if I'd been smacked on the side of the head.

I was alone in that room for what seemed like hours. I'd sit for a while then get up and walk from one corner to the other. There was a window overlooking a small parking lot, a doctors-only lot, big cars, MD plates. The men who were coming and going all looked like doctors to me. It wasn't that they were well dressed or particularly dignified. They looked busy, as if they were making decisions while they felt in their pockets for keys. All that hustle and brains and Jim was dead.

Without warning then, Mrs. Scanlon walked in with her arm around Phyllis. I stepped back. Phyllis's eyes glowed large but her stare was blank. She had that erased look of somebody fast asleep. She moved haltingly, excruciatingly slowly, without sustained rhythm.

"Leave me alone here, both of you," she said. The ordinary sound of her voice shocked me. She might have been giving me a direction in the office.

Mrs. Scanlon took me to the nurses' break room and poured me a cup of coffee. We sat at a grimy metal table and talked about wearing pants to work, whether it was right or wrong. Mrs. Scanlon was all for it. In her line of work, with all the bending and stretching, pants made perfect sense.

I finished my coffee and was sent back to the room to ask Phyllis if there was anybody she wanted me to call. She said no. She wanted to be there when her boys came in from school. She'd make her phone calls after she'd told them.

If I were Phyllis, I would have been reluctant to leave. Step one foot out the door and it's official. You enter the world as it will be from now on, the world without him in it. I was the one crying as we stood in the two o'clock sun waiting for a cab, not hailing one this time, just waiting. Eventually one pulled over. The driver pointed at us, said, "You want me?" We got in and Phyllis gave him her address.

My father died five months ago in a hospital in Pompano Beach, Florida. When we walked out, my mother, my daughter, my brother and I, we hesitated in the parking lot, none of us sure for a moment, which cars were ours, how many we had there, who belonged where.

## Two

PHYLLIS'S house was a tidy Cape Cod, white with black shutters, brick steps up to the front door, wrought iron railings. Inside the air was warm and smelled faintly of laundry detergent, as if someone were folding clean clothes in the next room. Phyllis led me past an immaculate living room, vases and ashtrays in their permanent places, vacuum-cleaner swipes on the carpet.

Between the living room and kitchen there was a cluster of framed photographs on the wall. Behind Phyllis, unobserved, I was free to search out Jim in a family shot. He was smiling but his mouth was blurred as if he'd been talking when the camera snapped.

Sunlight poured into the kitchen through two large windows. Phyllis sat down at the table and leaned forward, crossing her arms and rounding her shoulders as if she had bad cramps.

"Maybe you should lie down, Phyll." My voice sounded croaky in the bright light and quiet.

She looked at me and smirked—that is one corner of her mouth tightened and she rolled her eyes.

"Is there something you want me to do now, Phyllis, somebody you want me to call?"

She shook her head impatiently and motioned for me to sit down. My not knowing what to do and making a fuss about it seemed to annoy her. There was something reassuring in that. Our workday dynamic surfaced for an instant and shored me up.

Phyllis rubbed her face with both hands. "I can't breathe in here," she snapped. "Can you?" She lowered the shades on the two windows then paused as if she'd forgotten what she was about to do. She rubbed her hands up and down her thighs, looked at her palms. When she opened the small window above the sink, I felt the breeze on my face and realized I'd been sweating.

She took a bottle of brandy from the cabinet over the stove, put it and two juice glasses in the table, poured. We finished our drinks without talking and I poured two more. Through the open window I could hear the click and spray of a lawn sprinkler.

"I'm not much of a drinker," she said. "Ordinarily. Maybe if we go out to dinner I'll have a sherry, something like that. You and Ralph drink a lot, don't you?"

I nodded automatically though I'd been caught off guard. That Phyllis was talking at all surprised me and I hadn't expected the conversation to come to a point, a direct question, so quickly. "We go out all the time," I said. "Once we get married we won't drink so much."

"Wait'll you have kids. You'll stop. You'll stay home most of the time and drinks at home become a big production. You reach a point where it doesn't even occur to you."

Her voice had a timbre, a richness, I hadn't heard before. At the office her words were clipped, precise. If her kids weren't due home, I thought, I'd drink with her until she could sleep then sit and read a magazine outside her bedroom door.

I looked up and she was sobbing without making a sound, the heels of her hands against her eyes. Her lips were stretched open, her mouth a wide frown. I remembered the pull of that kind of crying from when I was little, felt it in my lips, how it centers there and radiates. I got up and put my arm around her. She was heartbreakingly thin, I felt like a big strapping girl next to her. She pulled away and left my arm cool from the dampness of her dress.

I went to find the bathroom and Kleenex. A full box, pink like the tile, sat on the back of the toilet. I didn't want to go back to the kitchen right away, so I looked at myself in the mirror for something to do, occupied sufficiently by the brandy's effects and the heightened sense of myself I always get alone in somebody else's bathroom. I saw myself in character, the girl from work here at a time like this.

I put the Kleenex down on the table and Phyllis looked at me as if she wondered why I was waiting on her in her kitchen. "I'm going to make coffee," she said, getting up. "You want coffee?"

"I'll make it. You sit down."

She had a drip pot just like my mother's. I knew how it worked and was grateful for that. Just as the coil turned red under the kettle, the screen door squeaked open then banged shut. "Mom?"

"In here, Peter," Phyllis said brightly. She ran her hands through her hair and wiped her eyes.

Both boys wore short-sleeved shirts, slacks, and black leather shoes with laces. They had the picked-over look of kids just home from school. The bigger one, James, looked at the brandy suspiciously then turned to his mother. "How come you're home?"

"This is Marie, guys, Miss Russo."

They said perfunctory hellos. I smiled too broadly. "It's good to finally meet you two. Your mom has told me so much about you."

They looked at me blankly, mouths open. They knew their mother better.

"I'm going to sit outside for a while," I said. "Call me if you need me, okay?" I walked out without looking at any of them.

The roof cast a triangle of shade on the front steps. I sat down there. Children carrying bookbags and sweaters walked past in groups of two and three. Looking at them, I was sure I knew what kind of boys Phyllis's sons were, what place they occupied in the world of grammar school. James and Peter—their names sounded heavy and formal with loss in my head—looked like boys who ignored girls completely, had one or two boys like themselves for friends. Their handwriting was probably sloppy. They had trouble staying inside the lines and gripped their pencils too tightly. Better readers, girls mostly, would cough and squirm when boys like these read aloud.

The sidewalks in Phyllis's neighborhood were bright white and the trees lining the streets were only about five feet tall and spindly. Everything looked new and none of it seemed sturdy enough to bear the weight of a young man's funeral.

James and Peter would become the boys whose father had died. I'd known a few. Embarrassment, not sympathy, was what I'd felt for them, as if their fathers had humiliated them by getting sick and then dying. The kid's desk would be empty for a week or so but the news of the death would stand in for him, hold his place. Then one morning he was back, a little disheveled-looking maybe but otherwise just the same. For a while, a year even, I wouldn't look right at him.

The lawn sprinkler I'd heard earlier was watering a square

of new grass next door. The area was roped off with green metal spikes and white string. Each time the sprinkler rotated it sprayed a piece of Phyllis's driveway, creating a perfect arc of wet pavement.

The taxi had inched into the driveway, come to a slow stop. Is there anything more irregular, more portentous, than a cab on a suburban street? Ambulances and fire trucks at least have urgency going for them.

A whistle came from inside and grew louder and louder until it was a shriek. The teakettle. I didn't know what to do. Surely Phyllis would hear it and turn it off. It went on getting louder every second until finally, abruptly, it stopped.

The boys came outside wearing striped T-shirts and dungarees. They walked past me, went as far as the side lawn where there was a swingset and a ball on a rope on a pole. They stood there, shoulder to shoulder, and the big one put his head down.

## Three

I WAS drawn to Phyllis that summer. Her grief seemed stark and genuine; I moved toward it. My own life had more or less fallen in on itself. Nothing was working.

The job at Meyer Brothers was ground zero for me. I had graduated from college in May then taught second grade for eight days. It was after four o'clock on a Friday afternoon and the principal had his raincoat on when I went in to tell him I was never coming back. "Think of the children, Miss Russo," he said, a ruined weekend taking shape in his eyes.

I had been thinking of the children, all twenty-three of them, their primary color clothes, the sleep in their eyes. In more generous moments I felt sorry for my class because their teacher was not the smiling, patient lady they deserved. Their teacher chatted with them one minute, ordered them around the next. By the end of the first week, they were wary of me, slow to smile.

Everything about grammar school made me feel murky and sad. The down-sized desks, the forced wholesomeness, the construction-paper autumn leaves on the windows. If I stayed, I thought, I'd become one of those truly bizarre teachers who tear around the school, nursing private, paranoid agendas, railing at their classes behind closed doors. "I'm so sorry," I said, pushing my resignation letter across the principal's desk.

After a few weeks of feigned job-hunting in Boston—read the classifieds, walked the streets, never once applied any-where—I ran out of money and decided there was nothing for me to do but go back to East Paterson. More than a lack of money sent me home. In May a boy I'd been in love with and wanted to marry told me to forget it, just forget the whole thing. I'd given him the summer to come around. In August he moved, a disconnected phone, a new name on the mail-box.

I went home because I'd botched everything up. I'd been away long enough to dream up a romantic notion of home as a safe place where I'd be able to get my bearings. At least that's what I told myself at the time. Now I wonder. I had to know my failure as a teacher would hit my father hard. Maybe I wanted to feel the force of his disappointment firsthand.

My roommate in Boston, a nurse, got a big charge out of the idea that we were two career women in the city, high-spirited, ripe for adventure. Then I started walking around the apartment all day in my robe, licking peanut butter off my index finger. I didn't want to tell her I was leaving because I knew she'd be relieved. While she was at work I packed my clothes, left a note on the kitchen table promising to send money for my share of September's bills—I never did and this has always pleased me. I drove to New Jersey as if I were on a leisurely car trip, stopping often for hamburgers and chewing gum.

When I got home, my mother, father, and seventeen-year-old brother were eating supper. I took my place at the table, looked into my lap, told them I'd quit my job. Everybody was quiet for a moment and then my father started to yell. Was I crazy? What the hell had he sent me to college for? Did I think a teaching job was a joke, something to try for a week, and then throw away?

My mother glared at me and shook her head. It didn't matter to her that I'd quit my job. Things that didn't directly involve her didn't engage her one bit. But she took her cues from my father and since he was furious she acted furious too.

Only Chris was glad to see me. He leaned against the counter and smiled every time he caught my eye.

I cried and knew I was crying because my boyfriend didn't love me, because I'd been so inept as a teacher, because I was

back home. There is nothing like the sound of a parent shouting at you. The worst of the voices in your head bombards you
from the outside.

My father looked out the window and spotted my car, the
brand-new Ford Fairlane the down payment on which had
been his graduation present to me. He'd pulled up in front of
the house flashing the lights and blowing the horn. Then,
embarrassed by his own enthusiasm, he was all business when
he stepped out. He made me sit behind the wheel while he
explained the terms of the loan.

"Just how do you plan to keep up the payments on that?"
he asked.

I admitted September's payment was already overdue.

"The car goes back to the dealer tomorrow. You want to
act like a twelve-year-old, you get treated like one. Twelve-
year-olds don't drive brand-new cars. They walk anyplace they
want to go and you can goddamn walk."

I ran up to my room, my old room, but didn't have the
nerve to slam the door. I sat on the bed and listened to him
lecture my mother about what form their response would take.
I could hear his tone but not his words. It was managerial:
we'll do this but not that. Every so often I'd hear my mother's
voice and knew she was saying yes, Lou, right, of course, of
course not.

Later that night he pounded on my door but told me not to
open it. "Stay where you are. Do not open this door. Are you
listening to me?"

"Yes," I said, feeling stupid, my hand on the doorknob.

"If you think you're going to sit on your ass, goddamn lady
of leisure, you're wrong. Until you find a full-time job, you

are to do all your mother's housework. Vacuuming, washing floors, everything. See how you like working as a maid." He gave my door another punch, the period at the end of his sentence, then pounded off to his room.

I barely slept; the night became surreal. I felt large, seemed to take up every inch of available space in my twin bed. I thought of Bill C., one of my erstwhile second graders. He'd been left back, a tall eight-year-old among seven-year-olds. When it was Bill's turn to drink at the midget water fountain, he'd lean way over as if he were bowing. I thought about Marty, the boy who'd rejected me and started me on this downward spiral. I was starving but afraid I'd run into my father if I ventured out of my room for something to eat.

I considered my punishment gingerly. It was too humiliating to face head-on, which was, of course, the whole point. To my father, my actions had been self-indulgent, theatrical. His response was designed to cut me down, make me understand that life was not about addressing every unhappiness that presented itself. Life was about work and shouldering responsibility no matter how shitty you felt inside. The punishment was engineered to deflate whatever sense I had of myself as earnestly negotiating with the world. His reading me so accurately infuriated me. I'd get my revenge, I decided, by being a good maid, making him think I planned to be his domestic for the rest of my life.

Our house was small, so I couldn't actually clean all day. Most of the time I walked around town aimlessly or lay on my bed but I made it my business to be doing some intrusive chore, washing windows or ironing in the parlor, by the time my father got home in the afternoon. He tried to ignore me but a couple of times I caught him staring at me mournfully from the end of the hallway or foot of the stairs.

One day I slept past noon and woke up to an empty house. My mother was out and I was alone. I savored the quiet, walked around drinking cold orange juice and waking up slowly.

When my father came in, I was still in my robe, just sitting down to a roast beef sandwich and a big glass of milk. To make matters worse, I'd found goblets of chocolate pudding, my father's favorite, in the refrigerator and had one out so I wouldn't have to get up after I finished my sandwich. My father made himself a Spartan cup of tea, sat opposite me, sipped it noisily. He looked at me and said, "I never thought you'd be the one to disappoint me." I steeled myself against his words, ate my sandwich, put the pudding back untouched.

The next morning I read the classifieds in earnest, called the employment office at Meyer Brothers, was told I could come in that afternoon. My mother softened when she saw me in a dress and stockings. "Marie," she said, "you're wearing lipstick!" I ignored her, went around her.

At Meyer Brothers I was given a tour and introduced to Saul and Phyllis. I liked both of them immediately, his manic energy and rapidly blinking eyes, her steadiness. She looked at him with a combination of disparagement and affection. "Don't pay any attention to him," she said when Saul had gone upstairs. "It's not a bad place, really. We do our work, nobody bothers us."

# Four

BY five o'clock Phyllis had been put to bed and her house was full of Jim's family. The women wept loudly and embraced and stayed that way for whole minutes, one's head on the other's shoulder. Jim's mother, a big woman with a lacquer-hard hairdo, kept demanding to know why she hadn't been called to the hospital. Daughters and daughters-in-law fussed over her, listened and nodded their heads. Everybody called Jim Jimmy. The boys sat watchfully at the kitchen table, eating grilled cheese sandwiches that were made for them by an older cousin, a girl they seemed to know well and like. The men—I couldn't pick out Jim's father—talked on the phone and stood with their hands in their pockets, looking over people's heads out windows. I waited for a chance to use the phone, called Ralph at work, went outside to wait for him.

Ralph is six-five, 250 pounds. People used to tell him he looked like the young Orson Welles. He had this overcoat, I remember, heavy tweed, full cut, the largest single garment I've ever seen. It was too bulky to wear while he drove so he used to lay it across the backseat then ask me to get it as we pulled in places. I'd turn around and there it would be, stretched flat in the dark like a refugee. I'd kneel on the front seat, grab the monster with both hands, and heave.

I can give you adjectives about Ralph—he was dependable, kind, cranky when things didn't go his way, marriage-minded—but I have to work hard for those. What comes easily is the memory of kneeling on the front seat, the waistband of my skirt pulling as I grabbed that overcoat by a lapel and a sleeve.

His car, a dull black boat, crept slowly down the street toward Phyllis's house. He was leaning over, checking house numbers.

I got in, pulled the heavy door closed, leaned over to kiss him. The instant my lips made contact I burst into tears, the kind of thing that happens when you've had a rough time and it's over and someone loves you. Ralph rubbed my back and said okay, okay.

We pulled away slowly. I put my forehead against the cool glass of the window, looked back at Phyllis's house. There were cars lined up in the street. A yellow light burned on the porch. I turned away, sat up straight, crossed my arms. We rode in silence for a few minutes. I knew Ralph was monitoring me, listening for crying. "I'm starving," I said. "Can we go someplace and eat?"

We went to a bar, a comfortable place with dark wood tables and dim lights. Ralph held my hand while he ordered steaks and gin and tonics. He asked how old Jim was. "Thirty-eight," I said, knowing exactly because Jim's mother had said it over and over. Ralph shook his head, rubbed the place just below his collarbone.

The food was delicious, hot and salty, and the din of the jukebox made conversation optional. Every so often Ralph leaned forward and asked a question, had Jim ever had heart trouble, how come I'd gone to the hospital, but for the most part we just ate and looked around.

By my third drink Phyllis and her tragedy, the hospital, her mother-in-law wiping the kitchen table over and over, seemed discreet and distant, like something that had happened years before. I was just drunk enough to miss a beat. This may be the allure of any drug, its ability to free you from the drudgery of one second after another. I wanted to stay where I was, inside the hum and the dim light where there was an endless supply of icy drinks with limes in them, where I could reach over and put my hand on Ralph's knee, where condensation beaded up on my glass and ran onto the shellacked wood of the table.

When I got home, my father was up and getting ready for work. He took one look at me and said, "Where you been?" I told him and he said, "Jesus, Jesus Christ." He made tea, shaking his head while he filled the kettle, biting his bottom lip as he put tea bags in the cups. He seemed angry at a world that would let a young man drop dead, and sorry that I'd been there to see it.

I sat down at the table and told him about waiting so long in that room in the hospital, about how Phyllis had looked when the nurse brought her in. He looked down at his teacup, at his own hands. "All right now," he said. "It's late. Get some sleep."

I was lying on my stomach when my father came into the room. I smelled his cologne, Lilac Vegetal, felt his awkwardness, feigned sleep. He started to pull the covers up over my shoulders, lost his way with that, cupped the crown of my head in his hand.

## Five

THE next day I went to work as usual. Of course I did. Jim hadn't been my husband or father or brother. Still, I would have liked to get out of bed at eleven or twelve, hungry, thirsty, shored up by sleep, eat cornflakes and drink cold juice then wander the streets, letting what had happened settle.

All day long people I didn't know, women I'd only seen on the elevator, stood on the stairs and asked questions. The first few times I told the story I was honest, gave details, meant what I said, but then I began to wish people would leave me alone. Saul called me upstairs, closed his door, told me to have a seat. He leaned back in his chair, wrists limp. "I couldn't sleep," he said. "I kept thinking about Phyllis and how everything changes for her now."

Around three o'clock I put my head down on my desk. All day long I'd looked at faces animated by the news of Jim's death, ghoulish under fluorescent lights. Phyllis's empty chair kept taking me by surprise. It looked like her the way an object, a shoe or a coat, comes to resemble its owner. I cried on the street waiting for my bus and wondered why I so rarely saw other people crying in public. It seemed to me I cried in plain view quite often. When I got home, I changed my clothes then walked over to Arnie's, a garage where Chris worked on cars he was fixing up to sell.

A car the exact color of Comet was up on the lift. Chris stood under it, his back to me, staring up at the hollow where the right rear tire should have been. "Come on, babydoll," he said softly. "Where is it already? Where the fuck is it?"

My head cleared for an instant. There's something savory about catching your brother talking to himself. The malicious delight is automatic, left over from the time you and he competed for a place on the couch, came to blows over a graham cracker. He was always there, the other fish in the bowl.

"I'm here," I said, "so stop talking to yourself."

He smiled, took a lawn chair down from a nail in the cinder-block wall. "Sit while I finish this one thing and then I have something to show you, something you won't believe, something beautiful."

"I don't want to see anything beautiful. I'm not in the market. Strictly ugly things today if you don't mind."

He looked at me over his shoulder.

"I don't want to talk about it. I came down here to watch you work is all, to find spiritual sustenance in the quiet dignity of your labor."

"Right."

The webbing of the old chair was soft and, to a person desperate for solace, soothing. Within a minute I was crying again, moved by the dimness of the light, the earnestness of Chris's raised arms, the smell of grease and damp concrete. "You know what happened to me yesterday?"

"Huh-uh," Chris said, reaching up with one arm to spin a metal disk.

"A lady at work's husband died of a heart attack and I was there. I went to the emergency room with her and he was dead when we got there."

Chris stepped out from under the car and stood with his

arms at his sides. In one hand was the light he worked by, a device that always made me think of a grenade.

"He was thirty-eight. I keep thinking how any of us, you or me or anybody, can die anytime. You pick up the phone and a voice says I'm sorry but so-and-so is dead."

Arnie, the owner of the garage and Chris's mentor, chose that moment to come inside and say what he always said to me: "How's school, sweetie?"

"Fine," I sobbed. "How's everything with you, Arn?"

"Fine, fine," he said, hurrying into his office.

Chris washed his hands at the sink. He scrubbed them with a brush and some pink paste then dried them carefully. "Come on," he said. "Come and see what I bought."

I followed him out back to the shed, a freestanding structure of corrugated tin. Chris took keys off his belt and opened a padlock then struggled with the door, lifting it up and over high spots in the macadam. He switched on the overhead light and I saw it all at once. A red Corvette, a convertible. Astonishing. I'd expected a nice car but couldn't believe this machine, this big-nosed piece of business here, belonged to my little brother.

"Where'd you get it?"

"I bought it."

"How much?"

"Too much, don't worry."

But I was worried. I was already thinking about what my father would say when he saw it. He prided himself on driving nondescript economy models. When a neighbor called him outside to admire a new Buick or Oldsmobile, he went eagerly, grinning and shaking his head. This red flash would infuriate and repulse him. I ached for Chris because I knew in some misguided way he'd bought the car to impress the old man. I wanted to ask if Dad had seen it but didn't. I was proud of my brother for going out in the world and getting a Corvette for himself. My father the ascetic could wait.

"Let's take her out," Chris said.

"I can't. Ralph's picking me up at seven."

"Call him. Tell him you're sick, tell him you have some business to take care of."

Chris pulled out fast and the back of my head hit the seat. I'd never been in such a snazzy car. The seats were soft but solid, close to the ground. The inside was small like a cockpit.

We drove up to Harriman, a reserve of mountains and lakes thirty miles north of Paterson. Chris looked puny behind the wheel; the expanse of hood seemed like too much car for him. I was uneasy and felt as I had when we were much younger and doing something daring like rifling through the strongbox my parents kept under their bed, each tapping into the other's nerve.

When we were a good way into the mountains, Chris pulled over and said, "Your turn."

I started out slowly, wanting to get the feel of it, and the feel was good, like driving a regular car on black velvet. I'd always been impatient with the cars I'd driven, leaned forward in my seat to urge them on. This car was impatient with me. It wanted to go faster and surge by surge I let it. There was no time to think. The curves were coming at me and the straight-aways were here and gone. All I could do was perfectly matched with all I had to do. The car on the road. My hands on the wheel. Chris, his profile handsome and serious, beside me.

## S i x

THE day after my father died Chris and I followed an under-taker through the unmarked door into a coffin showroom. It was not unlike a car dealership, caskets of metallic blue and mahogany and plain black parked at angles, a card listing fea-tures and ending with price beside each one. We went to a rectory and talked to a priest. A florist summoned us to his cash register by calling for the Russo children, my middle-aged brother and me. We stood silently in the doorway of my par-ents' bedroom while my mother selected clothes for my father. We stopped at the hospital to get my father's dentures even though the undertaker told us he could work without them.

By three o'clock we were finished. We sat around the living room of my parents' condominium eating bologna sandwiches and drinking beer. Chris told Rita, my daughter, about the Corvette he'd had when he was seventeen, about the day he and I had taken it out. "You should have seen your mother," he said, sliding down in his chair and making that closed-mouth shifting-gears sound. Rita beamed at Chris—she'd had a crush on him since she was two or three—then rested her head on my mother's shoulder. I'd asked her to take care of her grandmother while Chris and I were out making funeral arrangements and she'd done so with tender focus. A few days later my mother would brag to a couple of the women in her building: "My granddaughter, my shadow."

Chris sat beside my father's hospital bed day after day. I made several trips down during the year he was sick but never stayed more than a few days. "Hi, Dad," I'd say, and then I'd talk compulsively about whatever news I'd heard on the radio of my rented car, about Rita's progress in college. I knew how proud he was to have a granddaughter at an Ivy League school, had listened to him explain the difference between Penn State and the University of Pennsylvania to the men in his retirement community. My father was dying and I was still playing to his desire that his family achieve academically. Chris was at the hospital so often he could sit without talking.

I was grateful for Chris's devotion. If he hadn't been there so much, I couldn't have been there so little, but at the same time it made him strange to me. I'd always had the inside track with my father. Suddenly the alliance was theirs. I had trouble meeting Chris's eyes when he'd take me out into the hall or down to the coffee shop to fill me in on the latest word from the doctors.

One evening I said good-bye to Chris and my mother at the hospital, caught a late flight home. My section of the plane was filled with Hispanic families who seemed not to have been able to get seats together. There was much visiting between the rows. Young men stood up, scanned areas behind them, waited to catch somebody's eyes, smiled and called out softly in Spanish. The lively atmosphere was welcome; I was restless from sitting around the hospital all day. When we'd been in the air for a half hour or so, I noticed there were several lone travelers like me, people in their forties and fifties who seemed to be heading home after visiting parents. Some, I was sure, had spent the day exactly as I had, put in their time in a hospital room. Our relief was palpable. We were getting sprung. We were shaking off Florida and our mothers and fathers.

I leaned back, took a deep breath, smelled Chris's cologne on my shirt. We were hugging a lot, at every hello and good-bye, letting each other know we'd find our way back once my father was dead. That afternoon Chris had run down a corri-dor, chasing one of my father's doctors who had stepped off the elevator and headed in the opposite direction.

Chris and my father used to argue in the middle of the night, my father getting ready for work, Chris just coming in. My father's voice in a full shout would wake me up. It would sometimes stop abruptly, become the sound of slaps and the dull thud of punches.

Chris never finished high school, which pained my father greatly. It wasn't that Chris had the ability and not the will. He had plenty of will. When I was in eighth grade and he was in fourth, I'd help him study for spelling tests. I'd sit him down at the kitchen table, literally push down hard on his shoul-ders, and browbeat him. "Fifteen lousy words!" I'd groan and pretend to faint. He seemed to think he had it coming. He wanted a A badly and figured I knew what had to be done.

The spelling tests were on Friday. After school on Monday I'd demand to see his paper. He'd bring it to me dutifully, sorrowfully, a big red F. "But you knew these words," I'd say, looking down at *definately* and *recieve*. "I know them until the second she says them. Then I don't know them anymore." His voice would be higher-pitched than usual and reedy. By the third of my eight days as a teacher I'd identified a Chris in my class, a skinny boy with watery eyes who fidgeted in his seat while he filled in nothing but wrong answers on his work-sheets. It would have been my job to stand over him and deliver F after F.

When Chris was twelve, he started hanging around Arnie's garage. I'd walk by on a Saturday and see him standing in the shadow of the Coke machine, timidly petting the German shepherd with the scars on its nose. By the time I moved back to East Paterson, Chris had become a skilled mechanic and a buyer and seller of cars. He made more money than my father, he told me, but what impressed me most was the way he conducted himself during business deals. My inept little brother had become slick. He said things like, "I'll sit on this for one more day, twenty-four hours, you understand, but then it's going." I liked to watch him work on cars. Once in a while he'd ask me to start the engine and then he'd listen so intently his eyes would lose focus. I'd wish I had some sort of expertise, the ability to hear distinct elements in a rush of sound.

My father had been forced to quit school at fifteen. "The Depression, nobody working, a guy had to offer me a job." He'd been a good student. "A natural reader and writer," my grandmother would say, and I'd see a flash of anger in my father's eyes. "People used to pay him to write their letters, Italian or English, either one."

For thirty-five years my father delivered milk for a tyrant, a man who fired people for mumbling, for not shaving, for wearing their uniform pants on weekends. Mr. Addleson once barged into our house to see if my father's ankle really was sprained. He found my father ensconced on the couch in the parlor, a bowl of chocolate ice cream in his lap. Caught living it up at home, enjoying his injury, my father was rattled. Mr. Addleson made him get up and pull back the blanket to reveal, lucky for us, an ankle swollen up like a grapefruit.

My father's dream of a different sort of working life for Chris survived all the F's and even the notice from school that Christopher would be enrolled in the sixth grade again in September. Left back. Chris suffered all summer waiting for his sentence to begin. For the next several years he stood an unhappy giant in the back row of class pictures. When the money started to come in, when my brother began carrying a wad of bills in the front pocket of his black jeans, my father had to face the truth. He did so cruelly, never missing an opportunity to express his disappointment. He was unfailingly rude to Chris's friends, boys like Chris who drove down to central Jersey on weekends for stockcar races. Whenever Chris talked about a car he was working on or selling, my father made sure his impatience with the conversation was clear. He'd look as if someone were explaining the details of some very bad news.

I sniffed my sleeve greedily. Chris's cologne was nice, made me think of a well-dressed man walking through snow-covered woods, but I'd been telling him for years he wore too much of it. That afternoon my father had insisted that Chris and not the nurse help him into the bathroom. He'd leaned on Chris meekly, told him the nurses were all in a hurry, weren't worth spit. Chris said, "Take it easy, Dad. All right? I'll do it."

A stewardess came by with the drink cart and I ordered Scotch. A man stood near my seat, waiting for the bathroom. He was in his late forties, tanned, prosperous-looking. Three little girls ran down the aisle toward him. They wanted to use the bathroom too and stopped where he was, giggling, teasing each other in Spanish. They were in the midst of a game that involved slapping each other on the knees and repeating one phrase over and over. He watched them for a moment then leaned against the partition, put his hands deep in his pockets, swallowed hard. For all I knew he was worried about the cocaine stashed under his seat but at that moment, for me, he was the son of dying parents. He'd done what he could and now he was going home, taking brutal images with him—an old man refusing to eat tapioca, teeth clenched against the spoon—staring up at the ceiling while little girls played at his feet.

## Seven

JIM'S funeral was on a Saturday, two days after my ride in the mountains with Chris, and Ralph was still mad. I'd left him to sit on the couch and drink glass after glass of orange soda on an empty stomach while my mother said, "She *was* here," and swung the proof, my purse, slowly before him. "And the whole time your father's smirking, walking around in his pajamas at seven o'clock at night."

Church. What better place to play the supplicant? Timidly, I looked over at Ralph, from his knee to the knot in his tie. He held on to the pew in front of us with both hands. Ralph always did that, sat down and held on. In the passenger seat, at the movies, in his favorite chair, Ralph grabbed hold, as if he had to, as if we all should. I ran my index finger across his knuckles. He didn't respond but an hour before he would have pulled his hand away or, worse, jiggled it brusquely.

So many people at the funeral looked like Jim, had his blue

eyes, his hairline, his way of standing with his arms crossed
and head tilted to one side. His brothers were the most obvious.
One, in particular, could have been Jim's twin and he seemed
sheepish, as if he knew why people looked and then looked
again. There were also women and old people and clusters of
kids, all unmistakably blood relatives of Jim's.

Taller, blonder, skinnier, Phyllis was so clearly not one of
them. She wore a royal blue dress, which surprised me. (This
was ten years before people stopped wearing black to funerals,
a misstep if ever there was one. How can you be expected to
stand in the same room as the coffin of somebody you love,
stare hard at the place where his face must be, imagine his
eyes closed in the absolute darkness—for a moment, you and
he, the dead he now, are the only ones in the room—how are
you supposed to get through this in a yellow dress? When you
look down and see what you've got on, your liver or brain or
pancreas would have to secrete a month's worth of something
in protest, to hell with homeostasis.) I wondered if Phyllis's
blue was circumstantial. Was she too pale to own a black dress—
in black she'd look like a newspaper photograph—too tall and
skinny to borrow one, too busy these last days or too dis-
traught to go out and buy one? All of the Macdonald women
wore black.

A young minister stood behind the coffin with his arms raised.
He had thinning red hair and black glasses. He seemed nervous, preoccupied with his performance. At first his voice was
soft and low. He talked about God's plan, God's mysterious
plan, the perfect order that existed beyond the realm of human
understanding. Then he shouted, "Whosoever believeth in me
shall never die." Jim, he said, wasn't granted length of days

but he was granted depth of days, whosoever believeth in me shall never die. We can make Jim immortal by perpetuating the good he did here among us, whosoever believeth . . .

Church never lives up to my expectations. I want something otherworldly; what I get is ordinary. The priest at my father's mass had a head cold and sneezed seven or eight times. This minister seemed to know he was sinking, delivering only the standard fare trumped up with awkward theatrics. His delivery became more and more frantic until he was flinging stuff out at us ". . . a reason for everything, earthquakes and fire and disease . . . a time to be born, a time to die."

Phyllis sat dry-eyed amidst the weeping Macdonalds. She looked up at the ceiling then down at the heads of her sons. I quake to think what it must have been like for her to listen to religious slogans three days after the heart in the chest of her handsome young husband had stopped.

The minister's remarks came more slowly. Finally in a regular voice he said, "Let us pray. Our Father . . ." When he was finished, he stepped to the side and Phyllis made her way out of the front pew and up to the lectern. People turned to each other and whispered. Ralph looked down at me and raised his eyebrows. I slipped my hand into the pocket of his jacket.

Phyllis looked out at us like a principal at a school assembly waiting for students to quiet down. When the murmuring and the coughing and the sound of women crossing their legs stopped, she said, "I made some notes," and held up an index card dark with writing. "At five o'clock this morning I sat down at my kitchen table and made a list of things I might say here." She looked down at the card, one side and then the other. Phyllis was a listmaker. At work she always had a couple going, letters to write, supplies to order. In the aftermath of Jim's death, Phyllis had made a list.

"On Wednesday morning at ten o'clock Jim was at work. He was standing in the hallway talking to his boss, Jack Beatty." Her eyes rested for a moment on a man near me, a solid-looking guy in his fifties who looked back without flinching.

"It was then that Jim collapsed. A vein in his heart ruptured. He died twelve minutes later in the ambulance on the way to St. Joseph's Hospital in Paterson."

After so many years this scene is clear. Phyllis was telling the story, saying out loud what had happened. All of us in the pews were rapt. We wanted to hear it from her. There was that peculiar jolt the news of a death brings. When a famous person dies, you hear it on the radio or see a headline and even if it's somebody you never thought much about, Hubert Humphrey or that man who held on so long with the artificial heart, you're stopped for a moment, stopped.

"What I thought I was going to talk about, what I've written down here, was Jim's strengths, the kind of man he was. But you all knew him in your own way. Nothing I say here will tell you anything more about him. Jim died on June eighth at ten-twenty A.M. Today we bear witness to that. James Allen Macdonald is dead."

She pinched her lower lip and looked over our heads to the back of the church. She was working to hold herself together, straining but managing. All she said then was thank you.

I fell in love with Phyllis at that moment. No matter what else ever happened between us I knew I would love her for standing so straight and talking about her death in words that offered no comfort. I wanted to be with her, sit beside her, feel her ruthlessness and her courage.

I called Phyllis two weeks after my father's funeral, hadn't spoken to her in years. "My father's dead, Phyllis," I said. She said, "Oh, Marie," and then was silent for a moment. "You tell me about it. Right now. You tell me all about it."

At the cemetery she looked scarecrowish and weary. Her older son held her hand dutifully. The other boy, Peter, watched everything that was going on intently. He examined the mound of displaced dirt and then the coffin. A teenaged boy cleared his throat loudly and Peter sought him out and stared. He looked at the temporary awning, support poles, canvas, rope, and fringe. I knew I was watching him make some of those disturbingly vivid memories we carry out of childhood. Right now, I'll bet, he remembers that pile of dirt and the peculiar gloss of the fringe but doesn't have a clue how he felt that day they buried his father.

## Eight

"THE family invites all of you back to the Macdonald home for a luncheon," the minister said when it was all over and we went, Ralph and I, because I wanted to see Phyllis.

I left Ralph by the door and made my way through the crowded rooms. In the hallway I turned to edge past a group of people and found myself looking right into the photographs on the wall. This time I looked hard at Phyllis. It must have been Easter. They were standing on the front steps of the house. She wore a gray dress with a white bow at the neck, a hat, and white gloves. In the kitchen I asked one of Jim's brothers where Phyllis was. "She went upstairs as soon as we got here," he said. "She's had it."

Phyllis's bedroom was brightly lit, which threw me. I'd expected lights out, maybe one small lamp burning. Phyllis sat on the unmade bed still wearing her raincoat, her legs crossed, one foot bobbing.

"I just wanted to check on you."

"Here I am," she said dully.

She didn't invite me to sit but I did, carefully, on the edge of the chair the way you do when you want to assure somebody you won't stay long. I was determined not to talk, not to make her talk. I planned to sit with her for a minute then go.

Her head dropped to one shoulder and then the other. She rubbed a corner of the sheet between thumb and index finger. "He was still warm when they brought me into him. I put my hand on his chest and it was still warm but then he started to cool. I had to slip my hand into his armpit or under the small of his back to find a warm spot then.

"He looked like he'd been in a fight. Jim used to get in fights all the time before we were married. His lips were cracked and sore-looking and his hair was wet. He had red marks on his neck and chest like somebody had grabbed him hard. His skin was gray, that part is true, but he didn't look anything like he was sleeping. You always hear dead people look like they're asleep. That's a lie. He didn't look anything like he was sleeping."

RALPH was at the foot of the stairs talking to Saul. They'd recognized each other and stuck together. Saul was tastefully dressed, dark suit, white shirt, striped tie. "How is she?" he asked, and his expression went flat as he looked toward the top of the stairs. I told him she was exhausted, said I thought she'd be relieved when everybody went home. "You'll call her tomorrow, Marie?" I said I would and the three of us walked out to our cars. Saul hugged me before he got in his. I hoped Phyllis had seen him so somberly dressed.

Ralph and I went back to his apartment, a converted basement beneath a two-family house. Ralph's apartment always reminded me of a fort, a place kids claim and furnish with stuff swiped from their mothers. The light was dim, the tile cool, the ceilings just inches above Ralph's head. He had a bed, a card table and two folding chairs, a few towels, no bath mat, kitchen stuff he'd picked up in the supermarket. We used to eat cereal out of coffee cups, spread butter with a paring knife.

It was an enormous relief to be there, just the two of us, after a long day in dress clothes, a day of public ceremony and private jolts that had left me blurred and headachy. I took off my dress and shoes and stockings, leaned against the counter in my slip while Ralph, without his shoes or jacket or tie, with his shirtsleeves rolled up, opened two cans of chicken noodle soup, added just one can of water, and put pats of butter on top of Saltines.

Before picking up his spoon, Ralph reached over and pulled my chair closer to his. He could do that smoothly, without straining. This was the sort of action that was permitted when we were alone, action without forethought, explanation, reaction.

## N i n e

RALPH had come along during my murky period. I was spending days in that windowless office and nights in my room. A girl I went to high school with introduced us. I ran into her in Woolworth's, where I used to spend a good part of my Saturday afternoons wandering amidst water pistols and perspiration shields and brands of cold cream nobody ever heard of. I felt at home there. When Patty found me, I was examining a boxed set of underwear, each pair embroidered with a day of the week. Saturday was black with red writing, Sunday white with gold. I was reflecting on the manufacturer's faith in the order of things when Patty said, "Marie, I didn't know you were home." She invited me to a housewarming party she was having that evening. I had no intention of going, said maybe I'd stop by.

That night I lay on my bed and wondered what the hell had happened. One minute, it seemed, I was a fairly hip college student with a boyfriend and the next I was meditating in the aisles at Woolworth's. I thought about Marty and wondered how it was that he had disappeared from my life without a trace. I wanted to know where he was at that exact second with an urgency that hurt and made me roll onto my side.

Downstairs my father was yelling at my brother. "I want you in this house by ten o'clock on school nights, midnight on weekends. This business of running around all hours is going to stop. You hear me?" Chris stormed out, my father went after him, I forced myself up and into the shower.

After years of college parties, loud music from a record player and girls throwing up in the bathroom, I appreciated the adult feel of this one. There were trays of hors d'ouevres and a tidy bar. The men wore jackets. I noticed Ralph immediately because of his size. He looked gentle and patient the way big men sometimes do.

We looked at each other for a moment and then he came over and introduced himself, shook my hand. Ralph has always been blessed with social grace. He performs all duties, introductions, good-byes, with ease. I often remain at gatherings longer than I want to because I can't bring myself to go around saying good night. Ralph can tell a three-minute joke and hold a dinner party rapt, make toasts, say bon voyage to people. He never understood my awkwardness, thought I was merely rude. "What are you making such a big deal about?" he'd say. "Just go over there and thank her for the flowers." "Come with me," I'd say, or, "You do it."

Patty came by and gave our conversation the hostess's sanction, insisting we sit on a two-seater wicker contraption that rocked. We wedged ourselves in and I soon felt as if I were being interviewed. Ralph asked me about my job, college, where I lived. He, I found out by ending each answer with its complementary question, was an engineer, worked for Marcal Paper, had graduated from Rutgers.

He didn't ask for my number but asked only if it would be all right to call me. That seemed gallant and I said sure. I was primed to meet somebody like Ralph. Here was a full-fledged adult man, steady and sure. The boy I'd loved in college was skinny and frenetic, rarely called when he said he would, laughed like an insane person, something I'd had to ignore in order to fall in love in the first place.

On the night before graduation he called just after my parents arrived and said we had to talk. I left before my mother was out of the bathroom. My father was still draining the cooler. An orange and some ham floated in cloudy water. Marty had become increasingly active politically during the time I'd been his girl friend. That night he told me needed a woman who believed in the struggle. I was, he said, parochial. *Parochial,* I thought, having only heard that word used as the opposite of *public* before *school,* what's he saying?

He told me he'd never really considered me his girl friend, had slept with many, many women during my tenure, pointed to my anger as evidence of my provincial approach to life. He said, "Sexual exclusivity doesn't interest me."

I didn't leave. No, that's not exactly right. I did walk out, got as far as the street, turned around and went back. He opened the door and looked at me as if to say okay, you understand the terms, and what happened then has remained a pocket of humiliation for me. I'd like to say it was passionate, bittersweet, sex on the edge of pain, but it wasn't. It was Marty looking almost bored, his hand on my shoulder pushing me slowly down. I got through it by splitting myself in two. There was me and there was the girl letting herself be pushed down.

The next day was ninety-two degrees and my graduation gown smelled of dry-cleaned perspiration. My parents weren't speaking to me. I'd come home that morning to a note on the kitchen table. "It's one A.M. and we're going to our motel." No salutation or signature. Their anger turned to worry when they saw the state I was in. My father watched me carry a full bowl of sodden Froot Loops to the bathroom to dump. "You're hung over, is that it?" he called after me hopefully.

They walked me to the gym, one on either side. I stopped to get a drink at a water fountain and had just lifted my head when I spotted Marty walking toward us. His gown was unzipped and billowed around him, the gold sash of the law school hung rakishly over one shoulder. He walked right past us without even looking at me. That moment can still make me open my eyes wide in the dark.

AFTER Ralph and I got married, he went to work for Ford and we moved to a suburb of Detroit. Not far from our house was a trucking company named Therman, Marty's last name. I'd be poised to pull out onto the highway or staring idly out the window of a diner, maybe I'd be pushing baby Rita on the swings, when one of those trucks would roll by.

The universe is not random. It's much worse. Can it be entirely coincidental that the boy I watched get thrown into a Dumpster of incinerator ash in sixth grade—he came out coated with white dust, he gagged and spit—the boy who went through thirteen years of public school without a single friend, was named Donald Solo? I went for a ride in the Everglades after my father's wake. When I stopped for gas, the attendant leered at me then said, "Awww, you look like you just lost your best friend." Did I have to move to a place where the name Therman in red letters ten feet high sliced across my line of vision every couple of days?

Ralph filed for divorce but I ended the marriage. I withdrew from it over a period of years, stopped going to Ford picnics and Christmas parties, made excuses to get out of the house at night, joined a bowling league, took ceramics. The pear I made, smallish and olive green, sits on my dresser now, a reminder of how miserable I was then. Ralph tried to keep things together. He'd sit me down and talk to me, he'd whine, demand, say, "Don't do this, Rie. Please don't do this." Then I started sleeping on the den couch and he said, "If you go, you're not taking Rita."

She was sixteen when I moved out. The first night in my own apartment I sat on the floor amidst boxes and bags and knew I'd done the right thing. I'd always felt like an impostor as a wife. None of it came naturally. The shabby apartment felt more like home than the house with three bathrooms ever had. I told myself that Rita would be there a lot. I'll probably see more of her now, I said. It didn't turn out that way. Rita was rarely there and when she did come she'd look at my things, my microwave oven and eyelet shower curtain, and roll her eyes.

AFTER Ralph and I finished our chicken soup on the night of Jim's funeral, we spread a quilt on the tile floor. I raised my

arms and he took off my slip, ran his hands over me as if it
felt so good. Ralph had this way of being passionate and completely himself that impressed me deeply. I wanted to tap into
it, learn how to be that way. Later he woke me up by holding
me, saying, "Come on, baby, I have to take you home." I put
my dress back on, dropped my stockings in my purse, leaned
against him while he drove.

I don't miss Ralph the way he is now, don't regret getting
out when I did, but if it were possible to go back to that apartment with its dim light and cool air, I would.

## T e n

A COUPLE of nights a week that summer I'd borrow a car
and drive over to see Phyllis after work. My father had sold
my Fairlane out from under me, so most nights I used Ralph's
car. Once Chris let me take the Corvette. Driving it on familiar streets, I felt none of the exhilaration I had up in the
mountains. It was vaguely embarrassing, like walking into the
supermarket all dressed up.

I want to tell you some of the things Phyllis told me that
summer but I don't want to have to go on and one about what
color blouse she was wearing when she said a particular thing.
Phyllis wore pastels. Imagine her in pale yellow or green. I
don't want to have to say that I walked in tentatively, sat
down on a couch, lit a cigarette, I don't smoke. I remember

plenty of that sort of thing and what I don't I could certainly invent but the thought of doing that makes me feel bone tired.

Before my time with Phyllis I thought death happened cleanly, thought you entered a separate realm where the death and its aftermath took place, where it was all by itself. I found out that death occurs in a perfectly ordinary context. All the regular stuff continues stubbornly around it. You still take showers and look for keys. The phone rings and you answer hello. The day of my father's wake we discovered that none of us, my mother, Rita, me, had panty hose to wear. I had to go to CVS and stand before the size chart to determine who needed A, who B, who C. I did it with a clear head. Here is what Phyllis told me in the weeks and months after Jim died.

Her dryer stopped working. It turned on and spun but there was no heat. She draped what she could of the wet laundry over the tops of kitchen chairs. The phone rang as she was hanging socks and bras around the rim of a laundry basket. While she talked, she looked around at her kitchen draped in towels and T-shirts. It looked eerie to her, like a house boarded up, abandoned.

She plucked her laundry from the doors and chairs, lugged it out to the car, drove a few blocks to a Laundromat. While the clothes were drying, she picked up a magazine, one of those Jehovah's Witness things that are always lying around Laundromats and bus stations. On the cover were the words *Do the Dead Know What the Living Are Doing?*

"I folded the clothes and said it over and over because I liked the way it sounded, the ordinary sound of *doing* mixed up with *the living* and *the dead*. It's stuck in my head now. I say it over and over and I wonder. Do you think the dead know what the living are doing?"

In the months since my father died I've been reading the experiences of other bereaved people, and, Christ, the messages they get. In their dreams the dead speak. "Don't buy me any more flowers, Carolyn. I have all I could ever want here." Sons and daughters smell cinnamon gum or White Shoulders. Widows feel warm spots on the couch. Red birds fly back and forth outside their bedroom windows. I was in the shower the other day listening to Ann Miller being interviewed on the radio. She told the story of doing a show with Mickey Rooney that included a number he'd always done with Judy Garland. She was about to go on when she heard rustling coming from behind a piece of scenery. She made herself still, waited. A voice said, "Annie, it's me, Judy, Judy Garland."

Tonight the sky seems especially vast overhead. The stars and the cold air and the sense I have of being all alone work together to create the kind of setting I think a dead person might choose. I brace myself and look up, dreading but ready and there is nothing. The night sky is perfectly mute.

Phyllis said there were times when someone or something interrupted her grief, when she had to work to maintain the appearance of widowhood but actually, inside, she was stockstill, 100 percent detached.

She had headaches like none she'd ever had before. The yellow and brown label on a bottle of Bayer aspirin still makes me think of her.

A widow friend of the minister came to see her. Phyllis hadn't wanted her to, had told the minister thank you but no. The woman came anyway. She sat in the living room and said widows need to talk to other widows. "She looked alcoholic to me," Phyllis said. "Veins in her cheeks and skinny legs. I knew I could never talk to her." The woman must have seen that she wasn't getting anywhere and without asking permission marched upstairs to Phyllis's bedroom. "You have to pardon me, honey. You have to let me do this much at least." She took a blanket off the closet shelf, rolled it into a long tube, put it vertically on the bed. "This'll keep you from rolling onto his side and the bed won't feel so damn empty." Phyllis said it did help—"How did she know which side was his?"—and was grateful to the widow for being so pushy.

"I get this feeling, it doesn't last, it comes and goes quickly, but just for a few seconds some part of me doubts the fact, the absolute once and for all business. I go over the whole thing one more time, review it in a couple of seconds, as if I might find a loophole, a glitch in the system."

The living and the dead. Makes them sound like segments of the population, respondents to a survey. Men and women, blacks and whites, the living and the dead. I began toying with the sentence, trying it out. I'd be at my desk opening mail and I'd say it in sync with the rhythm of my actions and think of Phyllis at home sweeping the floor or fussing with her hair and saying it with me. Do the dead know what the living are doing?

At nineteen Jim was arrested for reckless endangerment. Blind drunk on his motorcycle, he jumped a divider and caused a serious accident in which two people, a husband and a wife, were injured. The judge looked down at him and said, "The way you're going, friend, you're either going to be dead or in jail before you're twenty-five." At twenty-two Jim was drinking heavily, playing cards all night, hanging around with slack-faced men in their fifties. Then Phyllis backed into his car in a parking lot and left a note on the windshield. He pursued her for months. When she finally agreed to go out with him, he had a job and a car with a muffler. By the time they got married he'd become responsible with the fire of a convert. He insisted on buying twice as much life insurance as even his ambitious agent recommended. Phyllis remembered Jim's finger sliding easily down the columns of the table that listed premiums and payouts. "Five hundred thousand dollars," she said, and laughed dryly. "The money is good. I'm glad to have so much of it."

She had trouble sleeping, very particular trouble. She'd close her eyes and just as she'd feel herself begin to drift off she'd jerk wide-awake and have at that moment her only true understanding of what had happened, one human being to another. During the day she experienced Jim's death from her point of view, what it had done to her life, but at night it was Jim's death to Jim.

"Sometimes I like the idea of Jim somewhere, Jim thinking. Other times I say if you're dead, just be dead."

The body. Immediately afterward and for a few days to come there is the body at the center. Months later you know it is still there in the ground, the hands with the rosary, the suit and the tie. What minus what, the body.

"I hated the way he acted like the life he'd given up, the motorcycles and the drinking, was glamorous, as if he'd made some big sacrifice. Once he told me he'd never wanted any of it, not a wife, or kids, not a house with a mortgage. He said he'd done it all for me and I should be grateful, the son of a bitch, I'd say, and then I wonder if that's what made his heart stop."

A lot of nights I stayed with Phyllis until two or three then had to drive around until I was sure my father had left for work. It wasn't that he'd be angry at me for coming home late. As long as I was working and paying rent, ten dollars every Friday, my parents made a big show of treating me like an adult. I was sure it was all just another swipe at Chris. Him they were driving crazy with discipline. I didn't want to see my father at 3:00 A.M. because I'd feel churned up and tender from talking to Phyllis. One night he and I passed each other on the road, his milk truck and Ralph's black sedan. Neither of us acknowledged the other but I knew that like me, he was smirking in the dark.

When I was twelve, I wanted a lock for my bedroom door. In a cavernous hardware store, a hardware superstore, I chose one with a sliding metal bolt as thin as a pencil. All around me people were dragging sheets of paneling up to the registers, forcing fat rolls of insulation into shopping carts. Standing on line with just my lock in its cardboard package, I felt how small it was, suspected it wouldn't work.

The instructions said to screw one part into the wood of the door and the other into the molding, but my door was hollow and I was afraid it would split, so I glued the lock in place with rubber cement. I worked intently, got it just right, set it in the locked position to dry. My heart beat slowed; I took deep breaths.

Then my father opened the door. The glue gave out with no fight at all. He didn't even know the lock was there, had just come to tell me supper was ready. I said okay, okay, praying he wouldn't see the bolt and its receptor hanging stupidly from the door's edge. He didn't. I knew then that my father would always crash through, without even meaning to, and, worse, without even knowing he'd crashed through.

I've just come from a weekend visiting my daughter. She's a sophomore at the University of Pennsylvania, an engineering major, she has Ralph's head for numbers. She'd seemed so impatient with me and so big. This big girl is my daughter? Ralph's share of her tuition, the lion's share by court order, had not been paid and she railed at me over it in a restaurant. My Rita, who was the most placid kid I've ever known, if I said Rita, wear pants, Rita wore pants, sat across from me in a Japanese restaurant and said she didn't need the additional stress of late notices from the bursar's office. "If you and Dad want to play fucking games, that's your business but leave me out of it." The *fucking* was new and I shifted in my seat to accommodate it.

I felt hapless in the face of her anger, would have liked to tell her about the time my parents came up to Boston for my graduation, about spending the night with a boy who didn't want me while they sat up waiting for me. You're entitled to despise your parents, I wanted to tell her. What I told her was I'd call Ralph about the money. His new wife always answers the phone and her voice gets sharp and thin when she realizes it's me. Ralph pays but pays slowly.

When Rita was nine, my parents insisted I send her down to Florida for two weeks. Let us have her to ourselves, they said. Three days into it my mother called at midnight and said maybe it hadn't been such a good idea. Rita was miserable and wanted to come home. Put her on, I said. There was a pause and then Rita: "Can you come get me?" I flew down the next morning. In the cheesy and dank Fort Lauderdale airport Rita waved solemnly to me from the escalator.

Now I stay in a hotel I can't afford to impress her. So many of the girls she goes to school with come from rich families and she always brings one or two along. After an initial period of cordiality, every move I make, every word I say, rankles her. What I didn't know when I felt what she's feeling, when the sight of my parents made the muscles in my legs twitch, is that the feeling is mutual. You can't help but despise your grown kids. I'd sell my soul for an hour with the nine-year-old Rita, wish she were here with me now, solid in her quilted robe, round head against my breastbone when I hug her.

Phyllis said, "I worry about my boys. I'm afraid they've lost me too. I have no patience with them, don't want them near me. I shoo them outside right after breakfast, make them get out and play. No sooner have they walked out the door than I want them back again so I can start making it up, treating them better. When they come inside my good impulse lasts for five minutes and then I can't stand to be with them again."

She found half a roll of peppermint Life Savers in a drawer. Jim chewed them when he'd tried to quit smoking. She brought it to her nose, sniffed, put out her tongue and tasted, went back to bed, stayed there all day.

The shirts Jim wore to work were red, bright red, and there was a spot on the kitchen wall that was pink because he'd leaned against it every night after dinner, keeping Phyllis company while she washed the dishes. "I'm leaving it there, the pink spot. When I noticed it today I went right for my sponge. To leave it there would be morbid. No shrines. But I can have it if I want it. Nobody has to know. What am I supposed to do?"

From the kitchen window I watched Phyllis's older boy bang the hell out of their swingset with a two-by-four. He was wearing a bathing suit that was too small for him and his feet were filthy up to his ankles and he was whaling away on the glider, putting big dents in the metal. I was about to call Phyllis over, thought better of it, and turned away.

Later that night Phyllis and I sat outside drinking gin and bitter lemon. There was no moon or stars. When it got so dark we couldn't see each other's faces, Phyllis switched on the outside light. She sat back down and immediately spotted the ruined swingset, rushed over to it, ran her hands over the dents. "Who would do something like this?" she said and started to cry. "Who would do this?"

## Eleven

AT first Ralph was very understanding about my spending so many nights with Phyllis. He was involved in a big project at work, had to come up with a way to muffle the machine that wraps paper towels in plastic, worked late more often than not. Industrial muffling was to become Ralph's specialty. "Area of specialization," he would snap. "I'm not a chef, for Christ's sake." Once the project was finished, however, he started to complain.

I told him Phyllis needed somebody to talk to. "Why you?"

"Why not me?" "It's morbid, the two of you sitting around talking about death night after night. She doesn't need to sit up drinking and going over it and over it." "How do you know what she needs? Are you a psychologist now?" "I should be if I'm going to be involved with you. You only worked with this woman. Since when are you her best friend?" "How else do you become somebody's best friend? You're not and then you are."

An accusation lurked beneath the surface of Ralph's grumbling. He knew it and I knew it. Ralph had what I can only describe as a vague notion that I wasn't entirely heterosexual. This current ran through our relationship without melodrama. There were no sudden realizations or revelations. The idea would occasionally come up is all. I'd watch a girl cross a street and turn to find Ralph watching me. Even now I think he's waiting for me to settle into a comfortable, middle-aged lesbianism.

Ralph was curious about me the way he was about everybody who mattered to him. He didn't have conversations, he conducted interviews. He was always trying to get a fix on people. He used to study me and it was flattering. I'd tell him everything.

One night we were at his apartment and he was asking me questions, stroking my stomach the way he used to from one hipbone to the other, his hand moving like a metronome. "Will you answer something honestly?" "Ask." "Have you ever been attracted to another girl?" I wanted to be honest and had never considered the question in so many words so I had to think about it. There was a professor in college I'd thought a lot about. She'd inhabited my brain for a couple of years. When I went shopping, I'd ask myself what she would think of the dress I was about to buy. But I hadn't wanted to have sex with her, I'd wanted to *be* her, so I was about to answer no. Then I remembered something I could tell him.

"I was eleven years old. Every Saturday my friends and I used to pack our bookbags and go to the library because it was the one place we could go without getting flak from our parents. Mine used to point at me and say to Chris, 'You see why your sister gets A's.' The library was in the municipal building then. It had a downstairs, a basement that was damp and had those little windows up near the ceiling. Drama books were kept there, drama and poetry. Nobody ever went downstairs. There was a little room off the main part, a meeting room or something it was."

Ralph's hand on my stomach stopped. I looked at him. It started again.

"I convinced my friends we should go down there and take off our clothes. We pranced around, told each other the librarian was coming, carried books under our arms, and said, 'I'd like to check these out, please.' The second or third time we did this we were sitting on the folding chairs making a big deal about how cold they were. I decided we should sit on each other's laps. A girl named Cindy sat on mine. She was tiny and bony like a little monkey with no hair. The other girls sat down so that they weren't facing each other but Cindy sat facing me. We started to move together, push against each other, and one of the girls who was watching made this noise, this humming sound. We kept moving, Cindy and me, and pretty soon we were all making the noise. Then one by one we stopped. It was perfectly quiet. We could hear footsteps above us.

"After that, whenever I was around Cindy, I'd feel this urge to take care of her. She seemed little and delicate and I'd want to put my arms around her. I used to ride her around on my bike, put her on the seat and I'd stand up and pedal. Then her father got transferred and she moved to Illinois. I used to look at her in our class picture, her skinny legs and her bright, beady eyes."

I NEVER resented Ralph's suspicions—they weren't even suspicions, they were inklings and they made me feel exotic. I liked it that he thought I was odd. I wanted a conventional life but I also wanted to be eccentric within that life.

I also had practical reasons for welcoming Ralph's grousing about the time I was spending with Phyllis. It gave me the opportunity to ask what his intentions were. I made my voice soft and serious, said, "Who are you to be asking so many questions anyway? We're not even engaged."

Ralph was dragging his feet, no doubt about it. When we'd been together just a few months, he had regularly alluded to the time in the future when we'd be married. He said we'd move into a garden apartment, buy a second car. I had put him off, said we didn't have to think about any of that yet. Somewhere along the way we traded places. The more he got to know me, it seemed, the less sure he was that I was the girl for him.

His reservations had mostly to do with my temperament. He didn't mind if I was half a lesbian as long as I was good-natured. Ralph said I was moody. Coming from him, that was a euphemism. I believe he was afraid my low-grade depression might flare up at some point and become full-blown mental illness. Also, the way my family conducted itself, the volatile nature of things in my house, mystified him. He seemed reluctant to get involved with people like us.

Ralph didn't volunteer information about himself, particularly past romances. I got him to tell me he'd been engaged to a girl in college. They'd dated for two years, got engaged one Christmas, and by spring had decided not to get married. The ring was returned without tears or raised voices. When I marveled at this, made Ralph describe the scene in detail, he got angry. "Everything that happens to you is not the worst thing in the world, Marie. Everything is not a catastrophe."

I felt I had to marry Ralph because if I didn't, I'd have to do something else. I suppose I could have bucked up, looked for a better job, got my own apartment, made a life for myself, but I didn't want to. I wanted to marry Ralph and move into a Cape Cod house like Phyllis's. I believed I was being sensible, forgoing the kind of intensity I'd felt for Marty, trying to marry a good man.

I proposed, in a manner of speaking, at the end of a long August day. We packed a cooler with beer and sandwiches and drove up to the mountains, my idea. Ralph went grudgingly. The woods didn't suit him. He kept looking all around and moved our blanket three or four times before he found a spot free of rocks. Ralph didn't own outdoorsy clothes, wore suits most of the time. That day he put on the pants and shirt he'd worn to paint his parents' house. He looked jaunty, there on the hilltop in his paint-speckled loafers and carpenter's jeans.

We had planned to go for a long walk but once we were in the woods we couldn't agree on what to do with the cooler—

I wanted to hide it in some bushes, he wanted to carry it with us—so rather than argue we set it down and forgot about going any farther. It was only about eleven o'clock and we weren't hungry but we ate because we didn't know what else to do. I planned to give Ralph an ultimatum when we'd finished and were stretched out on our blanket.

He had to lie diagonally to fit. That left me with a triangle of space and I curled into it. The sun was directly overhead and we were enjoying the novelty of being outside, the bright light, the hard ground, when I opened my eyes and found myself staring up at the indolent face of a little boy who took his fingers out of his mouth and let out a cry which brought his mother, a large Nordic-looking woman, crashing through the woods. Ralph, with characteristic presence of mind, grabbed the far corner of the blanket and pulled it over us. The woman dragged her boy away by the waistband of his shorts.

The mood was broken, my opportunity gone. We packed our stuff and drove farther north to Bear Mountain, an aging resort even then. There we rented a rowboat and took it out on a preposterously small lake. Ralph ran us aground several times with his vigorous rowing and cursed as he put his shoe in the brackish mud at the sides. When we were safely out in the middle, he took the oars out of the water and we drifted in the sun. I sat with my hands in my lap. I'd been dangling them over the sides until Ralph said, "Don't touch the water." I wanted to tell him we get married or else but couldn't bring myself to because if he said no, I'd have to endure being rowed back to shore unloved.

We had dinner in the hotel, asked for a table on the terrace. The sun was setting and there was a cool breeze. Ralph looked pleasingly tousled. His face was sunburned and sweat had dried in the creases of his neck. We ate slowly then drifted over to the lounge. In the center of the room was a huge stone fireplace in which, God knows why, there was a roaring fire. We sat on a worn sofa and were the only people who stayed put. Everybody else seemed to be passing through on their way someplace else.

We adjusted to the heat, gave ourselves over to it, even drank brandy. The softness of the couch, the warmth from the fire, the effects of a long day in the sun all worked on us. We drowsily groped each other.

Just as I was giving myself permission not to propose right then, to do it in the car on the way home, a bride in full regalia marched through the lounge. She was like a bride in a dream. She walked in a way that was completely unbridelike, all business, her train thrown over one arm. She was clearly a nudge from God. I sat up straight, looked Ralph in the eye, told him if we weren't engaged by September 30, we were through.

# Twelve

SAUL and I were swamped at work. The chute that ran from the mail room to my office was choked with envelopes. I worked as fast as I could and Saul came downstairs to help but got discouraged easily and either remembered something he had to do upstairs or wasted his time devising new systems to increase my efficiency. "I know," he'd say, uncapping his pen, "you make a separate file for each day's business." He'd write the date in his loopy script on the tab of a file folder. "Here's today's file." By the end of July the envelopes I pulled from the chute by the handful had patches of brown mildew on them.

Saul believed Phyllis would come back to work soon so was reluctant to replace her. I certainly couldn't do her job. At least once a day something would come up that I didn't know how to handle or had handled and botched, a customer complaint, a request from our sister store in Jersey City. I'd put whatever it was on Phyllis's desk and try to forget it.

Waves of anxiety woke me up between 4:00 and 5:00 A.M. In my bed I'd swear I was going in the next day to straighten everything out. I'd stay until midnight if I had to. Once in the office I'd make a few tentative moves toward organizing one thing then feel overwhelmed. Clerical despair would settle over me and I'd do what I'd done all summer: keypunch calmly while in the dark of the chute mold grew.

When I was in sixth grade, I walked around for months with a knot the size of an English muffin in my hair. It rested against the nape of my neck, hidden from view by a smooth top layer. I ignored it most of the time but was regularly seized by dread of the day my mother would discover it. I'd march home from school and shut myself up in the bathroom with every brush and comb I could get my hands on. I'd lay them out on the radiator like surgeon's tools. For five or ten minutes I'd work on the knot but it hurt; I'd give up and brush the top layer gingerly.

By August things at work were fouled up beyond belief.

Pounds of paper jammed the chute. The guy in the mail room just kept squashing it down. How different the sound that followed the creak of the metal door now. No more rustling of paper, just a sickening silence. Saul didn't come around much anymore and the phone rang constantly, its voices irate, nearly shouting. I wondered when the jig would be up, when I'd come to work and find security waiting to escort me out of the building.

At school one afternoon I just cut the knot out. I got my hands on the teacher's scissors—hers were pointed and sharp. Without a mirror I snipped until I was holding in my hand the thing that had burdened me for so long. It looked like a jellyfish, a central mass with tendrils.

I told myself that if Ralph married me, I could quit my job at Meyer Brothers, walk away from that nightmarish chute and the black telephone with its sputtering voices.

## Thirteen

I WAS a couple of blocks from home when I first smelled the smell. Oil burning. It was faint, there and not there, and I figured something was wrong with Ralph's black car. I got closer and the air was thick with it; the sky was getting lighter too, at midnight. It wasn't a blue sky or a gray sky or any blend of the two. It was distinctly brownish, completely unnatural, completely terrifying. Truck engines idled and car doors slammed as I turned onto our block and saw that the house four down from ours was on fire, the whole second story burning.

Fire trucks were lined up at the curb and firemen in yellow slickers shouted at each other and rushed past, their heavy rubber boots unbuckled. I could taste the oil smoke and the air was warm and ashy. People stood in the street and on the sidewalk watching.

Men stood with men and women with women, segregated, it seemed, by the nature of their reactions. The men were almost smug, almost smiling, as if they were thinking it isn't my house, poor son of a bitch, it isn't my house. The women seemed to be calculating the mess and the loss, their faces pale, their mouths open. They looked like hell, I remember, hair in curlers, no makeup, their husbands' sweaters over housedresses. All except for Mrs. Grant, that is, who lived a more glamorous life in the big house with the circular drive on the corner. She must have just come home from a night out with her husband, wore a black strapless dress and high heels. She stood in the center of the women, a deferential circle of empty space around her. I remember her impossibly delicate shoulder blades and the curve of her spine. In the strange orange light there was a tentative quality to Mrs. Grant's bones. She had bones like a rabbit's.

Word that I was there got to my mother in seconds. She hurried toward me, said, "Mr. Metuchen is dead, Marie. They carried him out a few minutes ago. Smoke inhalation we think it was. They carried him out right past me."

The Metuchens had lived up the street for as long as I could remember. They had no kids, which made them something of an oddity on the block, but stranger still was Mr. Metuchen's hair. In East Paterson, New Jersey, in 1963, Mr. Metuchen had hair to his shoulders. He wore it in a ponytail tied with a leather shoelace. I never knew what his hair was all about, if it had political or religious significance. If it did, it was the only sign of whatever devotion prompted it. Otherwise he was unremarkable. Tall, thin, watchful, a construction worker who carried a steel lunchbox.

I looked for my father among the men but he wasn't there. Had he chosen to stay inside for the same reason he refused to crane his neck when he drove past a wreck on the highway? Did he think it was vulgar to stand in the street and watch your neighbor's house burn? In the hospital, years later, he cringed at the exhibitionism of some of the other patients, refused to roll his IV stand down to the dayroom, and never discussed his condition with roommates. I thought of my father up in his room determinedly trying to sleep and listening intently in spite of himself. How could he stay up there when outside Mr. Metuchen was dead and Mrs. Grant looked beautiful amidst the smoke and the heat and the firemen?

The smell of creosote from the Metuchens' tar paper roof lingered all summer and I was troubled by an image of Mr. Metuchen burned, his bones specifically, a forearm or femur charred to a point like a log in a fireplace. The harder I tried to drive the image out of my mind, the more persistent it became until it lodged itself behind my ribs and I experienced it by feeling it, a visceral sort of seeing. I'd inhale creosote, feel the blackened-bone image, and be achingly aware of my joints, rub my thighs and forearms.

When Chris called to tell me a lesion had been discovered

on my father's right hip, he stumbled a few times on the word
*metastasized.* "It's spread," he said, finally.


WHEN I was seven or eight, I thought God looked like a
statue a teenaged boy in the neighborhood had made. It was
a stick-figure man, life-sized, made of some porous material. I
used to knock on the Goldsteins' door and ask to see it. Mrs.
Goldstein would stand at the entrance to their finished basement and wait while I took a good long look. The face reminded
me of the face of Jesus I'd seen in pictures and on crosses.
Whenever I thought about God—you do quite often as a child,
he's as real to you as the other stuff you hear about but never
see, operating rooms, the jungle—I pictured God as the statue
in the Goldsteins' basement. Except that in my mind God
didn't stand erect like the statue. In my mind God reclined
on one elbow and looked down at us languorously.

As I lay on my bed or stood on the sidewalk breathing creosote that summer, the image of Mr. Metuchen burned called
up in me the memory of the dark and pitted surface of the
God statue. Twenty-five years later the pair of images was
back—burned bone, apathetic comfortable God—dogging me
again, whenever I thought about the cancer in my father's
hip.


THE fire was out. Beneath a skeleton of collapsed beams,
the first floor of the Metuchens' house was intact. Chris and I
sat on the hood of Ralph's black car and watched the firemen

pack their gear. My father's truck inched out of our driveway but didn't stop even when a couple of men from the neighborhood walked toward it, expecting it to, wanting to hear what Lou had to say about the fire.

## F o u r t e e n

PHYLLIS made me tell her the story of the fire over and over, even said I should have called her. "I would have come over, I swear I would have." She asked how old Mr. Metuchen was and I said I wasn't sure, fifty or so. "Fifty," she said, nodding her head, as if I'd confirmed something she'd suspected. He, at least, was fifty.

I was glad to have something to offer that interested her. When I talked about Ralph or the mess at work, she seemed to drift, as if she had trouble following me. But her interest in the fire was endless. She insisted we drive past the house. "I just want to see it. I just want to see what it looks like." She stood on the sidewalk with her hands at her sides and looked up at it coolly like a city inspector.

She told me she was having conversations about death with all sorts of people, the woman in the estate tax office, her dentist, the seventy-year-old man she'd hired to cut her lawn. I felt a twinge of jealousy. She said, "I never knew how to talk to people about death before all this but I've learned one thing. You talk about death the same as you do anything else. Most people, people of a certain age anyway, have a story and they'll tell it if you ask."

When her newspaper came in the afternoon she turned right to the obituaries and read only those of people who had died young. She wished obituaries listed cause of death and resorted to figuring that out when she could by the charity listed at the end, the one people were asked to make donations to in lieu of flowers.

Now I ask people if their parents are still alive. Only those with two living parents are surprised by the question. I move on. Most people are generous with their information. They name the disease, describe the accident, tell me where they were when they were told. Grown children of dead parents tell you how old *they* were when the parent died. "I was twenty-seven when my mother died." "I was thirty-one." "I was fifty years old." Only occasionally do you hear how old the mother or father was.

I don't take people with two living parents entirely seriously.

Phyllis didn't want to go home after she'd see the Metuchens' house, so we sat in the parking lot of a Dairy Queen and I drank my lime Mr. Misty fast and my temples throbbed and Phyllis looked at the speedometer and said it would be one thing if you heard the news one time and absorbed it, took it in. The trouble is, she said, you have to hear it over and over, you have to say the words to yourself, Jim is dead, and it cuts fresh every time. My father is dead, I say when I'm stopped at a light or stepping into a hot bath. Dad is dead. Louis Russo is buried in a box in a vault in the ground. I know exactly how his arms are positioned. I know the expression on his face. My father is dead. Again and again I'm leveled by the news.

## F i f t e e n

SOON after the fire Chris disappeared for five days. My parents drove around for hours hoping to spot the Corvette, reported Chris missing to the police, were reluctant to say the word *runaway*. My mother called boys Chris hadn't been friendly with in years because we didn't know the last names of any of his current buddies. We didn't know some of their first names. "Marie, that boy Chris calls Action, what's his real name?" From my bedroom I heard my parents' voice at nine, ten, eleven o'clock, the middle of my father's night.

When Chris had been gone for two days, my father asked me to walk over to Arnie's garage with him. It clearly pained him to have acknowledge Arnie's existence, say his name, admit he'd paid more attention than he'd seemed to. I couldn't remember ever walking through the neighborhood with my father. We didn't talk; we were on official business.

Arnie was sprawled across the backseat of a car, sound asleep and snoring, his boots sticking out the open door. My father bristled and crossed his arms, all of his suspicions confirmed. He stared at the street as if modesty prevented him from looking directly at Arnie. "Excuse me," he said.

Arnie bolted upright, looking as bad as a person can look: sweating and grimy, wild-eyed, an imprint of the carseat across one cheek. He looked at me, guessed who my father was, said, "Give me a minute. Give me just a minute here."

My father treated Arnie badly, purposely intimidated him, implied by tone and demeanor that Arnie was to blame for Chris's disappearance. He acted, my father the milkman, as if he had to be careful around the garage, keep his arms close to his body, or he'd get his clothes dirty. Arnie made it worse by trying to please. He kept saying gee and it didn't sound like he ordinarily said gee. "Gee, I don't know where he is. Last I saw him was Thursday. He came by with his girl, that girl he's been with so much lately. You know his girl?" It cost my father dearly to admit he didn't know Chris's girl.

I felt vaguely guilty while Chris was gone. My parents jumped when the phone rang. My mother waited for my father to answer it. My father, who never answered the phone, took every call. Before I left the house, they'd ask me where I was going, when I'd be home. After a couple of days I stopped going out at night and so it happened that my parents and I were sitting in the parlor watching the six o'clock news when Chris pulled into the driveway.

My father stood up and walked outside. I turned to my mother, thinking she and I would join forces. Her expression was self-righteous. There was muted glee in the set of her face. She was hiding her enthusiasm for what we both knew was coming—bash his head in, she should have stood and shouted—under the guise of dutiful parenting. Worst of all, there was something coquettish about her hands in her lap, the trace of a smile on her lips. She was basking in it, her man about to fight for her, so starved was my mother for any sign of devotion from my father.

75

There was a girl in the car. She was older than Chris and pretty in a slutty sort of way. Blond streaks in black hair, frosted lips.

Chris got out of the car and his composure slipped. All of his recent accomplishments and the attitude that went with them fell away. He looked about twelve. "You son of a bitch," my father said, shoving him hard against the car. Chris recovered and stood stock-still, tears in his eyes, his hands at his sides. My father pushed and shoved and slapped him into the house. The girl, who looked like no stranger to scenes of this kind, of any kind, you knew she could handle herself no matter what, slipped out of the car and walked toward the street. She was wearing a halter made from a gauzy black scarf.

Inside, my father pounded on Chris, telling him between blows to his stomach and chest that he'd put his mother through hell. His mother, meanwhile, stood in the doorway to the kitchen, her hands in her pockets, and seemed to be losing her nerve in the face of a beating far worse than she'd bargained for. With the sickening thud of punches in my ears, I shouted for Chris to go, get out of here, enough, I was saying, enough.

Finally Chris swung and swung again, sending my father reeling into my mother's china closet. It teetered for a long second—everybody froze—I added my fervent will to whatever gravitational force was at work—and down it came. I never heard a louder noise inside.

The screendoor banged and Chris was gone. From the porch I watched the Corvette with the girl back in it pull away. I turned and the flat of my father's hand caught me on the side of the face. The force of the blow wrenched my neck and I was terrified, trapped, my back against the railing. "Open your goddamn mouth again I'll knock your teeth out."

WHEN Ralph pulled up, I was sitting on the curb exploring the tender region of my face, moving my jawbone up and down, side to side. He touched the sore spot with the tips of his fingers. "What the hell is wrong with him? Why did he hit *you?*" The explosions in my house baffled Ralph. His family was endlessly placid, a father who hardly said a word, a mother who ran the show, two married sisters. There was plenty of stuff smoldering beneath the surface, at least I thought there was, but there were no fistfights, no swearing. They beeped and waved when they passed each other on the road.

The Corvette was parked in the street in front of Ralph's apartment when we got there. It was dusk and Chris looked rattled and pale under the streetlights. A bunch of kids were playing kickball at the end of the street and he looked at them while he talked, his fingers trembling holding a cigarette, his knuckles scraped. Ralph looked at him with intense curiosity, even respect. I saw how much he would have liked to ask twenty or thirty questions. Here was somebody who had just punched his father in the nose.

The girl's name was Vicki. She and Chris sat on folding chairs while Ralph and I leaned against the counter. Chris looked at me while he talked, said he left because September was coming and he couldn't go back to school. He knew my father would never give him permission to quit, but he was quitting, that much he was sure about. I saw again how hard school had been for Chris, thought about the summer after he'd been left back, how he'd stayed in his room most of the time. "So I have to move out. He'll never let me stay home if I quit school, you know that." Ralph asked if he needed money and Chris smiled. "Money is about the only thing I don't need."

Vicki sat beside Chris, not saying anything at first but looking territorial, as if she wanted it understood she was an important player in all of this. They both chain-smoked and she was in charge of the cigarettes and lighter. She gave him one for every one she took, lit two in her mouth, put one in his hand. She wore a lot of a perfume that was popular then. It was girlish, simple and sweet, the way some middle-aged men thought a girl should smell.

I asked Chris where he would live. Vicki said she had an apartment in Hackensack and wrote the phone number on a matchbook. The Corvette had seemed like too much for Chris, too exuberantly sexy, and it was the same thing with this Vicki, her round rear end and direct gaze, her nipples visible through black gauze. There was a kind of strapping sexuality about her like that of people who matter-of-factly and with all good intentions keep silk scarves and baby oil in their night table drawers like so much scuba diving equipment in the garage.

They got up to leave and Vicki asked to use the bathroom which gave me a chance to walk out into the entranceway alone with Chris. It was dark there. The only light came from under the three apartment doors. I knew I'd never live with Chris again. That part of our lives was suddenly over. We stood facing each other in the dark and said we'd talk in the morning. He hugged me and I felt how tall he'd gotten. My head was on his chest and I was remembering the years when our place, his and mine, was fixed.

I spent the whole night at Ralph's, which I'd never done before. We went to bed right after Chris and Vicki left even though it was only about nine o'clock. We lay on our sides facing each other and I felt scared and shaky. I pressed myself against him, forehead, hips, thighs. He ran his hand down the length of my spine, pressing too.

We both fell asleep and later I woke with a start, realized where I was, and felt sorry for everything that had happened that day. My mother's wedding dishes had been in that china closet, and the flowered vase my father's relatives sent from Italy—Chris and I never considered ourselves related to my parents' relatives, especially the ones we never saw, the ones who were just blue airmail letters that lay around the house for a while and then were gone. My father's six-inch bust of Verdi had been on one of those shelves and the crystal butter dish we used on holidays. A plate with a picture of the pope on it, the sixties pope, the one with the little round head who looked like a newborn baby.

## S i x t e e n

PHYLLIS told me she had a hard time deciding what to wear that morning. She said she was only going to the supermarket, for God's sake, she should have put on any blouse, but she had trouble now making even the smallest decisions. "If I stop to think, I'm lost." The morning sky was difficult to read. It looked like it might turn out to be one of those unaccountably cool August days when legs and arms left exposed go blotchy because of the slight chill in the air. She put on a sweat shirt, finally, told James to watch Peter, headed to the supermarket.

Food-shopping both comforted and disturbed her. It was comforting because it was familiar. She began as she always had in produce and wound up, like always, in dairy, where she'd be seized by the old impatience to hurry through the check-out and be done with it for another week. She didn't, of course, buy the things she used to buy for Jim. He liked green olives in his salad, drank A & W cream soda, took sandwiches of Genoa salami for lunch. It was hard to see these products, particularly the packaged ones, looking so stubbornly the same.

Walking up and down the aisles produced a series of small, painful shocks that she had to attend to and then absorb. She remembered an electrified fence around a horse farm near where she'd grown up in New York State. She used to go there to feed the horses and would take a twig and run it above the wire, forcing herself to touch down now and then. The shock would jangle the nerves in her arm, make it go limp.

She pushed her cart around a corner and remembered turning that same corner when Jim was with her. He'd been boyish in the supermarket, would approach with something frivolous, popcorn balls in colored cellophane, pistachio nuts, and try to sneak it past her into the cart. Her grip on things as they are now would slip at moments like this and she wouldn't have been surprised if Jim had appeared, walking toward her, smiling sheepishly, with something they didn't need and wouldn't buy in his hands.

She could put whatever she wanted in her cart now. For

herself she bought the most expensive shampoo and Basis superfatted soap. James and Peter got coloring books and water pistols, gimmicky breakfast cereals, the one with the marsh-mallows in it, the one with pieces shaped like animals. It was only fair, she said, that they feel the money too. When the girl announced the total at the register, twice what it used to be, Phyllis felt as if she'd accomplished something.

Her spirits, bolstered somewhat by her cartful of bags, sank when she stepped outside into the heat and humidity. The day had declared itself. Her sweat shirt against her skin made her think of August afternoons when her mother would decide it was time to see which of last year's school clothes still fit. Phyllis would have to try on coats and long-sleeved dresses, sweaters and leggings, while her mother tugged on hems and jammed two fingers inside waistbands. Phyllis would feel ashamed for having grown so tall. She put her groceries in the backseat and pushed up her sleeves. She couldn't wait to get home.

She didn't remember driving off the road, which scared her more than the accident itself. Traffic was light, surprising for a Saturday. She felt grateful for this, as if she'd been given a small reprieve. She could coast along in the right lane without having to pay much attention. She drove under an overpass, remembered the dark then the light, and the next thing her car was scraping along a three-foot cement wall that ran in front of a shoestore. "Maybe you fell asleep for a second or two," I said. "You haven't been sleeping. You're exhausted." She looked at me crossly as if I'd said something impertinent or stupid. "No. Because I remember going under the bridge." I admired Phyllis's candor, emulated it in fact, but there were plenty of times it hurt my feelings.

She got out of the car hoping nobody had noticed. It seemed nobody had. No cars pulled over; nobody came out of the shoe store to investigate. The metal over the front wheel was badly dented, so much so that when she got back in the car and tried to go forward there was a savage scraping sound. She attempted to pull the metal out with her hands but couldn't.

"I just stood there looking at it and seething. I wanted the last three minutes back to do over again. I wanted to undo this latest thing before it got a chance to settle in and be real."

The groceries, she thought. How long would the milk and the meat and the ice cream last in the heat? Kneeling on the front seat she arranged the bags so that all the perishables were in one and took that with her as she walked up the highway. "I was heading for a gas station I thought was a lot closer than it turned out to be. Don't ask me why I thought carrying the milk and meat would make them last longer. I just took them with me."

The bag was heavy and cool. She carried it against her body. Truckdrivers blew their horns and the shoulder got so narrow in places that she had to walk on the yellow line, cars passing just inches to her left. "You see this, Jim," she was saying, out loud into traffic noise. "I'm driving into walls now, walking along Route Seventeen carrying groceries."

The ice cream melting in the bottom of the bag gave off enough liquid finally to soak through. The whole bottom gave out. Two cylinders of frozen orange juice banged one after the other against her ankle. "I bent down and tried to situate as much as I could in my arms." She started to laugh at this point, could barely get the rest of the story told. "Then I said

no more, that's it. I stood up straight-armed so that the hamburgers and pork chops I'd tucked under my arms fell away. I
left it all there for I don't know who, the ants."

We were sitting on her front steps. She leaned back and
closed her eyes, said the accident made her understand something. Grief reverses the ordinary proportions of inner and
outer life. Your thoughts and feelings and memories are what
interest you. What's happening in the here and now you hardly
notice. There is this chaos inside that distracts so completely
the next thing you know you're driving into walls thinking
about a horse farm that hasn't existed for twenty years.

## Seventeen

RALPH asked me to marry him on September 7. "I planned
all along to give you an engagement ring for Christmas," he
said. "You really didn't have to hold a gun to my head, Marie.
You just had to be a little patient." Not exactly the sort of
proposal I'd dreamed of—I don't believe he meant to do it all
along, I believe he did it out of a sense of being inextricably
caught up—but a proposal nonetheless.

He came over on a rainy Friday night so we could tell my
parents together. The atmosphere in my house had been tense
since Chris had moved out. My father barely spoke to my
mother or me, went right up to his room after dinner. My
mother was in a state of continuous low-level panic, waiting
for my father to explode. She hammered at him with small

talk, tempted fate, ended nearly all of her sentences with "Right?" to which my father would grunt or not respond at all. Knowing this, what did I expect? I expected my parents to transform themselves upon hearing my announcement into two other parents, the ones who would kiss me, shake Ralph's hand, break out champagne for a toast.

We had fish, I remember, fried fish. I looked at the brown paper on the serving dish and felt my stupid optimism falter. The air in the kitchen was damp from the rain and oily. My mother's face was flushed from the heat of the skillet and tense because of my father's surliness.

I was so nervous I couldn't think straight. I was afraid my parents would react badly in front of Ralph, and I've always had trouble carrying out contrived scenes like this one, being the girl telling her parents she's getting married. I was so jittery, so generally rattled, I overfilled my glass, tilted a full bottle of milk as if it were nearly empty. Milk spread across the table, dripped through the seam in the middle. My mother always responded to spills as if they were personal attacks. She got angry. "Oh, Marie! Oh my God," she snapped, jumping up as if something were on fire.

We had to lift our plates while my mother wiped under them. When we'd settled back down, Ralph said, "Marie and I are getting married." It came out sounding like a challenge. Ralph assumed a defensive posture in my house, walked around with an expression that said don't start any of your nonsense with me.

I looked first at my mother. She was looking at my father. He sliced into a piece of fish with his fork and said, "What's that?"

"We're getting married, Dad."

Neither of them said anything for a moment and then my father stood up. "Look," he said as if we'd been arguing for hours, "you can have your brother at this wedding or you can have me. If he's there, I won't be. Count on that."

He carried his plate to the sink and dropped it so that it clattered loudly. I'd never in my life seen him take his plate to the sink. He was operating on some supercharged level, trying to retain control by doing ordinary things, but he couldn't remember the way he usually got up from the table. He walked out then, not just out of the kitchen but out of the house.

My mother began clearing the table, her actions rapid and spiky. She picked up our three stacked plates then put them down hard. "Did you have to do this now, Marie? You know there's trouble with your brother. Couldn't you wait until things calm down? For once in your life could you think of somebody other than yourself?"

As was so often the case, I said to her what I was too afraid to say to my father. I told her she didn't have to worry, I didn't want her or my father at the wedding. They were barred, in fact, shouldn't even try to get in.

I was sobbing as I crossed our sodden lawn. Water soaked my shoes. I cursed wildly. Ralph took my hand and looked grim, as if he knew he had a repair job ahead of him.

We drove through one town after another. I cried and railed against my parents. After a while I began to notice the WELCOME TO and YOU ARE LEAVING signs. There was something soothing about them. When I'd been quiet for a few minutes, when we'd listened to the rain on the roof and the windshield wipers, Ralph pulled into the parking lot of a supermarket. He traced my eyebrows, nose, lips with his index finger. "I say we elope," he said and we did.

We were married in the mayor's office. Chris and Phyllis were our witnesses. She was waiting in the vestibule when we got there. She stood up, put her hands on my shoulders and looked right in my eyes. "Take a deep breath," she said. "Take a good deep breath."

The ceremony was brief. The mayor smiled while he said his part, Ralph's hand trembled as he put the ring on my finger, I felt how wrong it was for this to be happening without my parents there to witness it.

Ralph and I drove straight up to Niagara Falls. It was after midnight when Ralph insisted I climb into the backseat and get some sleep. His concern seemed husbandly so I did, used his enormous overcoat as a cover. I'd been drowsy but was suddenly wide-awake, listening to the engine through the carseat and looking up into the darkness. I was acutely aware of Ralph's presence, could hear him breathing, smell him in the collar of his coat. I was married to this man, oh my God, I was married. I knew he was thinking something similar. The air between us was thick with it. We were together now, him in the front, me in the back, not touching or needing to.

We stayed on the Canadian side of the falls in a beautiful old hotel. We slept late, ordered lavish room service breakfasts, went dancing every night after dinner. And, of course, we stood looking at the falls, walked alongside them, wandered out onto our terrace late at night to stand and watch. It's a shame newly married people don't go to Niagara Falls anymore. The ones I know, children of friends, all go to tropical islands. Right after you get married you don't need to lie on a beach, half drunk on rum in the afternoon, disoriented, headachy. You're much better off standing on a cliff where the wind is fierce and you have to strain to hear your husband's voice over the roar of the falls.


RALPH rode with us in the limousine to the cemetery. I knew it had cost him to be there. His new wife bitterly resents his ties to his old family. She'd made a stink about Rita's high school graduation party, refused to attend, insisted he stay only one hour. In the strange quiet of the limo—we were all exhausted by then, talked out—there was an embattled but determined look on Ralph's face, a look I recognized.

He'd arrived at my parents' condo unannounced, kissed my mother then Rita then me. I felt him looking at me with trepidation, as if he expected to find me gone to pieces. He and Chris stood on the terrace and talked while I watched through the sliding glass door. Middle age had softened their silhouettes but not otherwise changed them. They looked, in relation to one another, much as they had twenty-five years before. Chris was still lean and graceful, his hand in his back pocket, black leather boots on his feet. Ralph was still broad and still wearing suits and wing tips. He leaned in and said something and they both laughed. Just at that moment Rita, who I hadn't known was out there, came into the picture and stood between them. They turned slightly to include her.


IN the church parking lot, gravel crunched under the limousine's tires and I couldn't look out the front window because the hearse was there, silver not black, a curtain across its back window. I looked at Rita—her face was slick with tears—then over at Ralph. He was holding on to the seat in front of us with one hand and to Rita with the other. I moved over, wanting to feel her shoulder against mine.

At the grave we listened to a prayer in the bright Florida sun and said amen. Red flowers were placed one by one on the coffin and then it was the moment I'd feared more than any other. It was time to go. Ralph put his arm around Rita and led her to the car. Chris stood between my mother and me. We were gathering the will to leave him there, trying to come up with it between us. And we did, of course, lifting our heads and signaling to each other: now. Now. We turned and walked unsteadily across the soft graveyard grass.

# Hungry Dog

WE were scrawny, scrappy, not very pretty. We weren't the sort of girls boys in our high school flipped over. Up at the Hungry Dog it was a different story. Everybody loved us there. We went to work in short shorts, tank tops, Dr. Scholl's sandals that were supposed to make our calves shapely.

Our customers were all men, truckdrivers and guys who worked on the assembly line at the Ford plant. We'd look up and see a group of Ford workers in navy blue coveralls waiting for their chance to cross Route 17. When it came, they'd run all together. Eva said they reminded her of a baseball team heading out to the field. She'd nudge me, say, "Here they come."

The Dog stood in the shadow of Stag Hill. Jackson Whites lived there. They were a group of mulattoes who kept to themselves. We heard stories about inbreeding and truant officers being shot at with rock salt. The Jackson Whites who came into the Dog had kinky reddish hair and nervous eyes, paid with crumpled dollar bills and lots of change. It was 1975. We lived in a New Jersey town that was devoid of history—nobody's parents, even, had grown up in Montvale—and there we were selling hot dogs to the descendants of slaves who had been freed by Andrew Jackson.

Our friends worked in supermarkets and fast-food places with names everybody knew. My parents would have preferred if we'd found jobs like those but were glad we were working at all. I don't remember either one of them ever setting foot inside the Dog. When my mother had to drive us up there, she'd stop the car at the edge of the parking lot.

Eva and I couldn't believe our good fortune. Just fifteen minutes from our suburban home we'd stumbled on this pocket of tough guys in their twenties and thirties. The boys in our high school didn't thrill us. They were too much like us: sheltered, amorphous, soft. We all seemed to be standing around waiting for our lives to begin. Our customers at the Dog had declared themselves. The world had worked on them. They had calloused hands, heavy beards. Their blue jeans were darkened with grime from the road or the factory.

For a while we were in love with all of them. The way they rubbed their eyes after taking a first long swallow of coffee, the bandannas so many of them tied across their foreheads. One would chastise another for saying cocksucker or motherfucker in front of us. A truckdriver would come in dusty and bleary-eyed, go right to the men's room, emerge with his hair damp and freshly combed, the top of his T-shirt wet. He'd sit down, smile, say hey girls.

Then Bobby, a Vietnam vet with tattoos on his forearms, started bringing Eva jewelry from the Southwest, tough biker-girl stuff, a coiled snake with bright green eyes, a turquoise thunderbolt. She kept it all in a zippered compartment of her purse so my mother wouldn't see it. As we drove up to the Dog, she'd put it on piece by piece.

Eva began leaving the Dog to be with Bobby. As soon as he pulled in, she'd climb up into his truck with an agility I hadn't seen before. When she got back, hours later, she'd look pleasantly mussed, her dark eyes shining.

I liked being at the Dog without Eva. I'd lean against the counter and we—six or seven guys and I—would watch familiar sit-coms on the small black and white. I'd watched those same shows with my girl friends, even at home with my parents. Around eight o'clock we'd turn off the TV and drivers from Tennessee and Mississippi would argue with auto workers from Newark about which radio station we should listen to, country western or a black one that was all the way at the end of the dial. I liked being in the middle of that, knowing that Eva was out there in the night like a scout, riding around in Bobby's truck, wearing all her jewelry.

As was bound to happen, the headiness of close quarters, southern accents, second looks that shot straight through me coalesced into a crush on one man, Mike. He was neither a truckdriver nor a Ford worker. I didn't know what he did except that he drove a battered station wagon, one of those cars you see in parking lots, a tool chest on wheels. The backseat was permanently down to make room for ladders and push brooms. Crushed styrofoam cups and empty cigarette packs were sprinkled over everything like croutons on a salad.

Mike was in his late twenties, tall and lean, had a black man's mustache and beard. I think of him whenever I see a picture of Malcolm X. He had a sinewy intensity and sharp wit, didn't say much, hovered around the outskirts of conversations making occasional wry comments. I believed he and I were smarter than the others, made sure he knew I got his jokes.

Mike's skin was light brown like a Jackson White's, but I wasn't convinced he was one. Unlike them, he always came in alone. They were hicks, said dang and reckon, and he seemed worldly. Then one night a couple of them came in and, as usual, ordered their hot dogs to go. When they left, Kyle, a loud, stupid guy nobody much liked, started bad-mouthing them, calling them J.W.'s, saying they all had blood diseases because of incest.

Mike got up, walked over to Kyle, and just stared at him. Kyle's voice trailed off. He withered in his seat. Mike looked ready to swing. A couple of guys stood up in that call-to-action way men will when a fight is about to start. Mike turned and walked out slowly. He stood in the parking lot and I could see his shoulders rising and falling as he took deep breaths.

He started coming in every night. I was nervous around him because I'd spent so much time thinking about us. In my head our affair was progressing nicely. I'd anticipate his laugh seconds before it came and congratulate myself on knowing him so well. I interpreted everything he said to me as clear evidence of his attraction and began taking longer and longer to get ready for work. I'd emerge from the bathroom at home, eyes made up, hair blown straight, reeking of the Charlie I'd put on all my pulse points.

One night I was working alone. Bobby was on the road and Eva had begged off, said she didn't feel like being around people. The sadness in her voice hinted at the downside of all this, the treachery of love. Mike sat at the counter spiking his Cokes with rum he poured from a flat pint bottle and smiling at me in a way that seemed purposeful and sly. I could feel his eyes on me when my back was turned. The smell of his rum found its way to me through cigarette smoke and the salty steam of hot dogs. I wanted only to keep whatever was going on between us alive and knew I was doing all right.

Then I put an onion on the cutting board to slice. The knives had just been sharpened. I cut my finger, blood flowed. Mike saw it happen and straightened in his seat to get a better look. His eyes, my blood. It was a peculiar and intimate moment, like when you drop something and a stranger kneels to pick it up. He came behind the counter, soaked a clean rag in cold water, wrapped it around my finger, squeezed hard. The bleeding wouldn't stop, so I couldn't work. Mike took over for me, told people he was an emergency replacement and they should keep their orders simple. I had never seen such grace.

We closed at ten o'clock. Mike did what I told him to do, put the condiments away, turned off the steam table. He didn't seem fluid and relaxed the way he had earlier. His movements were taut and deliberate now.

Flirting with this man was one thing. It was something else entirely to be alone with him in a gravel parking lot on a summer night. The air smelled of exhaust from the highway and wet leaves from the mountain. My finger throbbed and I squeezed it, felt fresh blood seep into the napkin.

He leaned against the bumper of his station wagon, put his hand on my back, pulled me toward him, said, "You're just a little thing."

We kissed and a tremor went through me, a scalding sense that all there was was me. Now he'd find out I wasn't who I'd pretended to be. I'd kissed boys in the corners of basements and backyards but there'd always been other people around, some of them kissing too, girls smirking at each other over boys' shoulders. Mike's seriousness and plain desire were new. The kiss went on and on and I began to feel the pull of something genuine, something as simple and true as the ground under my feet. I could smell the Dog on us, the sour smell of coffee and fried onions that was in our hair, on our clothes. I put my arms around his neck. When I tilted my head, his followed. I was filled with a sense that my family, friends, school were all behind me. I was marching on without encumbrance. I thought of Eva climbing into Bobby's truck and felt party to that sort of momentum.

Then Mike slid his hand under my shirt and I froze. I had no breasts to speak of, a slight swelling was all, and the way my arms were raised minimized even that. I was sure he was accustomed to breasts with some heft. I stiffened, pulled back, was solidly in the middle of my own life again. Embarrassment revived fear and I knew I wouldn't go any further.

Mike looked at me for a moment then smiled and crossed his arms. "Go on home," he said. "You need to get in your mother's car now and go home." I did exactly that, drove with my bandaged finger sticking straight out. As I pulled into the driveway, I reached down to turn off the radio but in fact turned it on. It had been off the whole way and I hadn't noticed.

I hoped Eva would be awake so I could tell her I'd kissed Mike. She wasn't. I turned on the light in our room and still she didn't wake up. I took the spiral notebook I used as a diary out of my underwear drawer, looked around for a pen, spotted Eva's purse on the dresser. I opened the zippered compartment, scooped out the jewelry, put it all on. Looking at myself in the mirror, I brought my hand to my face so the snake bracelet would show. Eva stirred and I whispered her name. She nestled deeper in her covers, licking her lips and dreaming, I was sure, of the tattooed forearms of her Vietnam vet.

# What You Leave Out

AFTER a shower now I walk around wearing nothing but my bootee-style bedroom slippers. The radiators here blast heat but the floors stay cold. I jog down the hallway from bedroom to bath for exercise. I undress in the living room. All of my work clothes, my dresses and pumps, are finding their way to the hall closet.

Other people keep you in check. If, for example, you were to use a fresh mug for your second cup of coffee at breakfast, your husband or wife would object. You'd have no choice but to admit that refilled cups smell swampy and hope for understanding, which you wouldn't get, so you'd stop the nonsense, use one cup, learn to endure the brackish smell that makes you think of murky aquariums with every sip. When you live alone, you're free to indulge the palest preferences. You collect quirks like coins. Collecting itself may become a quirk. You may find yourself filling coffee cans and margarine tubs with quarters, dimes, and nickels.

I'm flirting with a younger man at least, a former student who walked into my classroom five years after graduation and asked me to read his stories. He calls me nothing, I've noticed, must be unsure whether he should stick with Ms. Duggan or come on over to Eileen. His work is lively and his thighs are long. I left my husband one year ago. The night I moved out he and I had gone to a party at the math teacher's house where we played Trivial Pursuit. After not answering a single question correctly all evening, Jack guessed the Spanish word for navy, armada, and won the game for his team. On the way home he told me he hated the sound of my voice when I'd had a couple of drinks. I called him a name, a fucking something. He took one hand off the wheel and with an awkward backhand punched me in the stomach. My twenty-three-year-old is writing a novel.

Now, according to the distributive ed teacher, apples left uncovered in the refrigerator give off a gas that makes everything else spoil faster. I keep a large bowl of of red Delicious on my second shelf and have noticed spinach and romaine lettuce go quickly so I'm conducting an experiment. I've covered the bowl with aluminum foil and am monitoring spoilage.

Walter comes over on Tuesdays at seven. Every week he brings five or ten pages of his novel and we discuss the pages he brought the week before. He's writing about his father, who he believes has had it easy. Money, a harmonious marriage, tall healthy children have all fallen into this man's lap. Good fortune, in Walter's opinion, has left his father unable to acknowledge trouble of any sort. The opening scene has the Walter character coming home to tell his parents he plans to drop out of college. The father simply refuses to hear what the son has to say despite being followed from room to room and told over and over again. The father's steamroller optimism wins out. The son goes back to school.

All day long my students watch me. I can't so much as take off one shoe or count the money in my wallet without some bigmouth commenting.

I read something in a women's magazine about what people are naming babies these days. Michael is the number one most common name for boys. Walter has unknowingly fallen in step with new mothers and fathers all across the country.

The romaine seems to be holding up better but the spinach still wilts in no time. When Walter told his father he wanted to be a writer, not a lawyer, his father said, "Good. We need somebody in the arts in this family."

Last night I opened a bottle of wine but Walter didn't go for it. He drank half a glass; I finished the bottle. Ordinarily I walk him as far as the outside door but last night I stayed with him right to the curb and there, over the roof of his car, asked him if he wanted to go out for a drink. He said no. He had to be up early the next morning, wasn't much of a drinker anyway.

*Stunned* is too strong a word for what I felt. *Stung* is better. The skin around my eyes hurt like a sunburn. I picked up Walter's wine and drank it as I walked down the hallway to my bedroom and back again. I won't sit on a kitchen chair unless I've got two cushions from the couch under me. On Sundays I turn the clock to the wall and run on estimated time until dark. The life I meant to lead when I left Jack was supposed to be shaped by larger forces, painted with broader strokes. When you look ahead, you see yourself living purposefully, you focus on the big picture, then you get there and you're busy arranging and rearranging the clothes in your drawers.

Drunk and determined, I went into the bathroom, put on eyeliner, mascara, lipstick. I worked styling gel into my hair and made it stand up like the hair of the girls in my classes. I grabbed my purse and headed down the hall, lost my nerve, made the left into the bedroom, fell asleep in my clothes, woke up this morning with mammoth dents in my hair, shifting planes like glaciers. Apparently alcohol will not play a role in this seduction. What does this kid think is going on here?

In the classroom today I was manic, said whatever came to mind, kept leaving letters out of words I wrote on the board. Students, the dumber ones anyway, love that. They jump on it with both feet. By late afternoon a sure sadness had set in, a vibration behind my ribs like a cat's purr but with exactly the opposite meaning. There is no place drearier than a classroom at four o'clock.

I don't like thinking of myself as a wife who got hit. It's a history I don't want but I see them on afternoon television and my story is not different. Talk shows used to be Mike and Merv sitting around with crazy Dr. Stillman and his eight glasses of water every day and Totie Fields. Now Phil and Oprah stand in the audience holding microphones. What happened next, Veronica? What happened next? It started with Jack bumping into me hard on his way out the door after an argument and I wasn't always standing in his way. Sometimes he had to do a dogleg exit to work me in.

I can't sleep unless the door to my bedroom is closed. I didn't know this for a long time, was waking up at two, three-thirty, four o'clock. Then, desperate for a good night's sleep, I closed the door, locked it, slept soundly until six.

The aluminum foil over the bowl is getting worn from so many openings and closings. The gas, assuming it exists, must be finding its way out and doing whatever it does to the vegetables.

After the collisions came one ripped blouse. Jack grabbed a

handful of neckline and pulled slowly down until the material gave. It was a summer shirt, 100 percent cotton from India, but still. I knew I couldn't do that to his shirt without both hands yanking.

So why didn't I leave after the first shot? When I was nineteen, I sat at a bar talking to a woman in her thirties. We discussed a mutual acquaintance whose husband hit her. I have no sympathy, I announced, for women who stay. What's wrong with them anyway? Are they so afraid to be alone? The woman I was talking to looked bored and said it should be that simple. "Do yourself a favor," she said. "Don't talk about things you don't understand." How could she find fault with my clear thinking? I would be a different sort of adult. I would be steadfast, I would be strong, I would stay with a man who pushed me down every couple of months. The five or ten seconds of violence has to catch up with you. It has to tap you on the shoulder like smoke in an old-fashioned cartoon. It has to say, "Well?"

I was sitting on a kitchen chair, directly on it, no cushions. Walter was on the couch. We were discussing the limitations of a first-person narrator, but distractedly. I was savoring the underwater feeling of carrying on so bookish a conversation while imagining placing my hand in the hollow of Walter's chest and running it down into his jeans. (Remember standing on the playground and trying to pat your head and rub your stomach at the same time?)

When Walter had turned me down for a drink, I told myself I'd misinterpreted everything. All he wanted was my editorial advice. My blood jumped when he stood up, paused for a moment as if to get his bearings, came over, and put his arms around me. I was finally belly to belly with this boy-man I'd wanted to kiss for months.

Skin rubs skin and you can't deny connection. Your brain tries to pull back and narrate but your body, having a lot more to offer at the time, won't let it. Shut up already, your nerve endings shout, and pay attention.

One of my window shades came crashing down yesterday and hit the back of my hand. As part of my regular afternoon adjustments (so many up, so many down, according to weather conditions), I lowered the shade in the kitchen but it wouldn't stay. I tugged on it gently over and over, lost patience, gave one savage pull, and down it came. The pain made everything else recede, so there were just my two hands, the hurt one and the one holding it. "You can stay down there now," I yelled to the ruined shade at my feet. "I've had it with you."

The type of boy I like to watch at school is not a star. He's not one of the boys the girls chase. He's loose-limbed, too tall for his desk, smiles whenever I look at him, is straight up and down from shoulder blade to ankle. I'd like it if Walter had been one of these boys but he wasn't. The truth is I've tried but can't remember much about him from those days except I have a vague sense he was a good student.

The experiment is over, results inconclusive. I want to see the red of my apples when I open the refrigerator, gas or no gas.

I'm lying in bed with Walter and he's talking about his father. It turns out the old man gets drunk every night. Now I believe he exists. Before, he'd seemed impossible. I'm picturing Walter's father sitting alone at a kitchen table drinking gin when Walter asks me about my marriage, how it ended, why. It is my intention to draw a line. We are not going to talk about this. I'm about to say what I've said to absolutely everybody else who wanted to know: Jack and I grew apart. We wanted different things. I've actually said these sentences. I can't say them again because the image of Walter's father and his gin is hanging over our bed. "My husband punched me in the stomach once. A couple of times he pushed me down." Walter gasps softly, not a melodramatic gasp but a short, serious intake of breath.

It's 6:00 A.M. now and Walter has just left. Wearing only my slippers, I put my eye to the peephole and watch him walk down the stairs. His shoulders are broad and his shirttail is out. I'm proud to have him leaving my apartment at dawn. When he's out of sight, I turn around, put one slipper in front of the other, shift my weight back and forth, take off running down the hall. When I'm really moving, I slide, up and over the doorsill and I'm in the bathroom grinning. Let me try that again.

# The Size of
a House

I HEARD it from Nina who heard it from Mary who heard it from my mother who wasn't putting the receiver down between phone calls to her six daughters. It was a race of the dialing fingers. I got through to Patricia.

"They sold the house," I said.

"You're kidding. So fast?"

"Yep. I just talked to Nina. A 3-M executive from the Midwest."

"Kids?"

"Four. Three boys and a girl," I said. "Nina's going to meet me over there in an hour. Bill bought a case of champagne and wants us all to come over and help him drink it. Want me to pick you up?"

"Three boys? That's weird. How old are they?"

"I don't know. You want to come with me?"

"No."

"No?"

Patricia said she wasn't going anywhere. She said she was tired and was going to bed.


WE'VE called our parents Bill and Jean since we were teenagers. It wasn't some dippy egalitarian thing. It was derisive, a way to see them clearly.

I COULDN'T convince Patricia to let me pick her up, so I drove over to the house by myself, got there first, sat at the table and watched the others come in. Nina brought her overnight bag, went right for the champagne, drank one glass and then another, said, "There." My father always said Nina could never bear to see anything end. He said she used to go into a decline on Christmas night. She'd spent most of the summer after law school in bed. The night before her wedding she sat up late, listened to all our old records from high school, and wept.

Mary walked in smiling. She seemed filled with the antic good cheer some people feel during a blizzard or hurricane. Her eyes were bright and she looked ready to start packing or take down curtains.

Patricia came after all. She wore a sweat shirt jacket over her nightgown. Without a word to anybody she went into the kitchen, made herself a peanut butter sandwich and chocolate milk, then took her place at the table. A few years earlier she'd been attacked on the campus of the University of Virginia by a hillbilly with a knife and even then had come away talking, talking. The prosecutor told my parents they'd have had a better shot at a conviction if Patricia had been less chatty on the stand. The night we found out the house was sold Patricia didn't talk or seem to be listening. She stared straight ahead, chewing forcefully. When she drank, she held the glass to her mouth for so long she had to breathe through her nose.

My parents weren't speaking to each other, so we got the story of the sale in parallel versions. Jean said the woman was already planning to do all the things *she'd* always wanted to do but never had. Knock down the wall between the kitchen and the dining room, tear up the carpet in the hallways, strip the oak paneling in the den.

I leaned over to Patricia, told her that once Jean had said she'd like to turn our house around, 180 degrees, so the front door would be in the back.

Patricia didn't look at me but smiled distractedly, politely even, then put the locket she wore around her neck in her mouth.

Bill said the husband was in shock. "Absolute total shut-down. The poor bastard can't believe the price of real estate in the East." He laughed a particular laugh—chin down, head shaking—one he used when commiserating with another man in a tough spot. When he pulled up behind a car with a drag-ging muffler, he'd laugh and lean forward to get a better look. "He's got it attached with a coat hanger, see?" When Mr. Santo up the street tried to avoid putting in a new septic tank by planting an elaborate rose garden in the saturated ground, Bill walked around laughing this laugh that seemed to say to other men, "We are in the thick of it and most of what we try will not work."

Bill and Jean have always had periods when they don't talk. Once they went nine months. They'd say things to us they wanted each other to hear. We'd be lying around watching TV and Bill would come in, stare fixedly at one of us, and announce, "The plumber is coming on Wednesday afternoon. Someone has to be here to let him in." Jean would walk across his line of vision to let him know she'd heard. We'd all nod our heads.

Once Bill had us outside doing yard work. Jean came out to the porch and yelled about how she had no intention of paying for her long-distance calls. "The phone bill," she said, "is your father's responsibility. I'll call anybody I want." We kept our heads down, kept weeding, until Nina stepped behind a bush and twirled her index finger at her temple. Somebody stifled a giggle which set everybody off. Bill said we could get started on raking now since we'd found weeding so hilarious.

We always acted like the not talking didn't matter, like we were going about our business just the same. The truth was it got into our systems like drugstore diet pills. We had to pick up the slack and did by becoming exaggerated versions of ourselves. We talked louder, laughed more, rolled our eyes, slid down in our chairs.

Bill toasted the new owner, the real estate agent, Midland Bank, and 3-M. "May they sell a lot of Scotch tape," he said and closed his eyes. Jean made a point of drinking during his toast, of putting her glass down just as he raised his.

Patricia pushed her chair back and crossed her arms. She looked up at the ceiling and then over Bill's head into the street. Nina was getting drunk and maudlin. She decided she wanted a souvenir and went around the room, champagne in one hand, picking up disparate objects, a pewter candlestick, an old metal dustpan, a picture of Mary on her First Communion, saying, "What about this? Or this? Hey, what about this?" Mary's glee had mellowed some but she still seemed to be rushing to accept this, to get it under way. Patricia looked the way I felt, stopped, stilled, perfectly quiet, waiting for something to hit.

She stood up abruptly, said, "I'm going. Bye, everybody."

"Wait a second," I said. "I'll walk out with you."

She held her nightgown up around her knees as we made our way down the steps to the driveway. The outside lights, all of them, came on.

Patricia said, "Dad," under her breath.

THERE are four years and two sisters between us. I'm older. She doesn't figure in any of my big memories. I know everything that's happened to her and she knows everything that's happened to me but nothing of consequence has ever happened to us.

She'd been a gymnast, could do flips and no-handed cartwheels and Russian splits. Sitting at the dinner table in a leotard and sweat pants, she looked like an exchange student. Once in a while a couple of us would go to a meet and sit awkwardly on the bleachers, but we never quite had the look of the other families. They seemed focused and patient. We'd end up having a conversation that had nothing to do with what was going on around us, Patricia or some other girl slamming around on the uneven bars.

DURING the weeks between the sale and the move, all of us stopped by the house a lot. We were supposed to be helping sort things out but actually did very little. We sat at the table while Bill and Jean packed up around us.

Bill had always been neat. He used to scrub the sink with Comet and Brillo. He regularly disinfected the garbage cans. When we were kids, he worked nights. Every so often we'd get off the school bus and smell bleach and know that when we turned the corner, we'd see all the garbage pails lined up on the porch. "You have to," he'd tell us.

He seemed determined to leave the house immaculate. Most of the time we were there, we could hear the vacuum cleaner, near or distant. One Saturday he was downstairs cleaning the basement. The sound of the vacuum grew faint. Patricia walked in and said, "He's out there vacuuming all our cars." Later Bill came inside and looked at us. Still holding the vacuum, he said, "My mother was a slob, my wife is a slob, and all of my daughters are slobs."

My sister Nina was the lawyer for the sale of the house. She and Bill sat at the table going over paper work.

"And the termite inspector?" she said.

Bill got up and put his hands on the back of his chair. Nina looked irritated. "Well? The termite inspector? When's he coming?"

"Oh, Wednesday morning, ten A.M." Bill looked like he wanted to have all the right answers to her questions.

Nina scribbled something on a yellow pad. "And what are we doing about the roof?"

The buyer wanted my parents to knock five thousand dollars off the price, the cost of a new roof.

"The way I figure it," Bill said, "this guy's just making a last-ditch effort to save himself a couple of bucks—*she* wants this place is what matters—but he's thinking he can make a . . ."

"Don't quibble about the small stuff at this stage, Dad. People are unpredictable just before closing. He might walk. Then we're back where we started and the market keeps getting softer. You really have to figure what your time is worth."

My father sat down and listened.

"You do what you want, Dad, but remember, you're risking having both this house and the condo on your hands at the same time. That could wind up costing you a lot more than five thousand."

He stared at her, his hand over his mouth. I hoped he was asking himself if he should take the financial advice of a girl who lost her wallet four times in one year.

"Okay," he said. "You tell him I said okay."

I heard him tell Mary and then Patricia about his decision to give in on the roof. Both times he said, "You have to figure what your time is worth on something like this." Patricia said it back to him, nodding. "What your time is worth."


I PULLED into the driveway during the week and there were no cars there except Patricia's. She was sitting on the couch in the living room.

"What's with you lately?" I said. "How come you're so weird?"

She smirked. "I've always wondered the same thing about you. Why is that girl so damn weird?"

"Come on."

"Promise me you'll never become a mental health professional. You'd send people screaming into the night." She sat up straight and opened her eyes wide. "She wants to know why I'm weird. Oh nooooooo." She ran across the room, waving her arms above her head, had real trouble stopping at the wall.

"Boy, your legs are still so muscly."

She turned around fast. "Look, I'm just sitting here. Just sitting here sitting here. You want to sit here too? That's fine. You don't? Go sit someplace else."

THE day before the move all six sisters were at the house. My mother sent a plane ticket to Lissy, the youngest, who was taking summer courses at Rice because she'd failed four courses her freshman year. A bad love affair with a local was what I heard. I looked at Lis and tried to imagine her tromping around Texas having man trouble and not attending classes.

Deena had driven up from North Carolina. She's just eleven months older than Patricia. When she walked in, Patricia went right for her, said, "Dee, take me for beer?" Bleary-eyed and grimy from driving, Deena said okay.

When the packing was finished, my mother sent out for pizza and I took beer out of the refrigerator. It reminded me of the refrigerators at college parties, stacked six-packs, no food.

It wasn't long before husbands and boyfriends started to call. We took turns saying it's for you and passing the receiver.

"No. No. I don't know when. Make hot dogs," Mary said then sat back down.

"You get rid of him?" Nina said and everybody laughed, my mother loudest of all. I think she would have liked to get rid of hers too but of course hers was ours and he got to stay because he'd lived in the house as long as anybody.

We were quiet for a moment and then Patricia said, "I just

can't imagine driving by this place and not being able to pull in if I want to."

"Here we go," Nina said. One sister covered her eyes with her hands; another shook her head. Lissy stood up then sat right back down.

Patricia opened three beers, went around filling glasses. When she got to me, she said, "Remember our Barbara Ann routine?"

She was twelve. I was sixteen and fat and determined not to be when school started again in September. Her gymnastic mats were set up in the basement. We worked on a floor exercise for one solid summer, all the other sisters screaming at us to *stop playing that record.* She devised a big finish, both of us down in splits. When we practiced, she'd stand over me, her hands on my shoulders. "Easy . . . easy," she'd say. I hadn't remembered, but I did now, the music, the smell of the damp basement, stretching stiff muscles.

Bill shook a Hefty bag open and folded pizza boxes down into it. He picked up beer cans, emptied the ashtray, headed out to the curb. Jean followed him, looking grave and determined.

For just a moment we were kids again, squirmy and embarrassed. Then Patricia said, "Oh, fuck it. Fuck them."

She started walking back and forth, her hand skimming the backs of our chairs. "Remember when Bill used to go to work in the afternoon and Jean wouldn't be home yet? Remember those couple of hours when nobody was watching us?"

I did, we all did. Bill would pull out of the driveway and the air would turn sweet. The house would suddenly seem enormous, the ceilings higher, the floors slicker, the carpets brighter. It would become like an island, with coves and paths, wide open places, no rules. The younger ones might put on Jean's makeup and costume jewelry to drink grape juice out of Waterford glasses. They'd pry open a can of paint, dip their fingers in. We older ones would smoke cigarettes brazenly in the kitchen, curse casually, invite boys in when we could get them. We'd point speakers at the windows and blast Van Morrison at the neighbors, "Wild night is calling. . . ." Only it'd be four o'clock on a Tuesday afternoon.

"Some days it would really take off. Remember when we wouldn't be able to get things under control in time and Jean would walk in to find all kinds of hell broken loose? In one second we'd be serfs again. We'd have to clean up our mess, set the table for dinner."

We were going, we were all together now and we were moving. We had the sound of our voices and the memory of weekday afternoons when the house opened itself up to us and was ours.

# Diamonds

HE gave her the earrings six years before he died. "I bought something for you today," he said, pulling a black velvet pouch from his shirt pocket. He reached over their dinner plates and put the diamonds in her ears. Admiring herself in the bathroom mirror, she decided she wouldn't wear any other earrings, thought, yes, simple diamond studs every day. Not once during the six years did she so much as misplace them. Then, when he'd been dead a year, she started losing the diamonds.

One morning she stood in the hallway outside her classroom and put a hand to her ear. No diamond. She squeezed flesh and then cartilage as if she might simply have felt for the earring in the wrong spot. Fear flared under her skin like a rush of fever that says you're sick, go to bed.

In a stall in the bathroom, she undressed, hoping it had fallen into a fold of her clothes. Standing naked on the tile floor, students' voices in her ears, she ran her hands over her breasts, waist, hips. Her own fingers against her own skin, distracting, vaguely surprising at first, then familiar and heartening.

The school day ended without anyone finding the earring despite the enlistment of students, other teachers, even the surly janitor. Alone in the car on the way home, she was free to cry, to look at herself in the rearview mirror at red lights, to put her hand to her mouth. She had so many times rested one of the diamonds against the tip of her tongue. When she held something that was his, she instinctively brought it to her mouth. She'd press her lips against his watch face, run them over the wide part of a tie.

Years before, when she was in high school, there'd been a car wreck. A boy was killed. He was half of one of those spectacular teenaged couples, a boy and girl who seem to stop being everything but lovers. They mooned through the hallways, fed each other french fries in the cafeteria; he cried in public when they fought. His car hit a tree at the end of her street. She came flying out of the house, found him dead, put her fingers in the blood on the dashboard, and tasted it. At school girls whispered this story to each other, their eyes reverent. When she'd been told—when her best friend closed her bedroom door and said, "You know what Peggy did?"—she'd been appalled, not by the physicality of it but by the enormity of the forces at work. Even then she'd known they could wipe you out, forces like those.

When she got home from school, she found the earring on her night table, which meant she'd only put one on in the morning. That scared her, made her feel the degree to which she was mimicking, and mimicking badly, regular life. Her leaving the house wearing only one earring was as unlikely as her walking out while the oven was lit or the water running.

Since his death, she walked with her shoulders rounded, afraid something inside would give way and she'd tumble over the wreckage into a place that was hellish, a place where she'd surely disintegrate. She imagined she knew this place, thought of it as where she was headed when, jolted awake, she flattened her hands against the mattress, sure she was falling. It was the place she was falling to.

She called her sister. "Tell me," her sister said. She heard devotion, felt it through the phone like a hand in her hand, but was silent. Telling wouldn't work. Can you tell a blizzard that blocks the front door? Can you tell a rape? Could the sixteen-year-old with blood on her fingers tell?

"We should go away," her sister said. "You need rest." So they went the next day to a travel agent, an older woman named Edie who said, "I was thinking a few weeks in Spain." Three days later she picked up a white cardboard packet marked "Travel Documents," took it home, spread its contents on the couch, fingered the tickets and transfers, the ornate Spanish money, the crisp traveler's checks.

Madrid yielded to her because it was not familiar. She and her sister spent their days sight-seeing. At the Prado their guide pointed with his sunglasses to paintings by Spanish masters. They shopped and sat beside fountains to write postcards. Walking across wide streets surrounded by people she didn't know, she felt pleasantly numb. This is easy, she thought. I can do this.

THEY had an 8:00 A.M. flight to the coast. The wake-up call was late, the cab early. As they pulled into the airport, she put her hand to her ear. No diamonds. A frantic phone call to the hotel, her sister at her side, rapt and ready to console. "Hurry, please hurry," she told the second driver.

The earrings had been turned in by a maid, were sealed in

a small envelope across which her last name was written in pointy European script. She tore open the envelope, shook the earrings into her palm, made a fist around them. She was afraid the diamonds might disintegrate. Disappear. She'd feel them go and when she opened her hand, they'd be gone. Standing in the hotel lobby, she vowed never to take them off again, not even at night, though the posts were long and when she wore the diamonds to bed, she'd wake up to an ache that radiated from the place where platinum hit bone.

A few days later she got up early, dressed quietly so as not to wake her sister, drank strong Spanish coffee until her heart raced, walked alone through raucous Torremolinos. She bought toothpaste and nail polish in an airy pharmacy with a smooth wooden floor. A boy with a bare chest and blue eyes smiled at her on the street.

Slowly, gingerly—she didn't want to jinx it by paying too much attention—she realized she didn't feel fragile. Since his death she'd felt unmoored, had needed to press against that girder inside that said you're here, you're in one piece. She'd been waiting for that to stop, to blow itself out, wanted only to feel better. That morning she knew the turmoil wasn't going to leave her like a fever breaking. It would stay but wouldn't always scare her.

She kept walking and the day grew hot. She bought a beer from a vending machine for the novelty of it, sat on a bench that faced the ocean, talked to a Moroccan woman who tried Spanish then Italian before settling into English.

When she got back to the hotel, she put on her bathing suit and, for the first time since she'd arrived on the coast, rinsed off in the shower beside the pool. Europeans did that, showered before swimming, but Americans didn't and she'd shunned it as something foreign and unnecessary, like the bidet in the bathroom. The spray was soft; she could feel the cool water and warm air. Lifting her hair so the water could hit her neck, washing under her arms. Intimate moves in bright light.

She dove in, swam laps until her arms ached, lay down in the sun. When her heart stopped pounding and her breath slowed, she reached up lazily. One of the diamonds was gone. Oh Christ, she thought, not again.

She retraced her steps up to her room, looked there without moving anything, her hands in the pockets of her shorts. She thought of how far she'd walked that morning. The diamond, so small really, could be on any of a dozen long streets. She went back down to the pool and swam along its bottom, running her hands over the cement while her ears popped.

She felt herself being watched. A teenaged girl in a blue bikini sat on a chaise lounge, her hands clasped between her knees, her eyes lively and concerned. They looked at each other with guarded curiosity, like children about to risk an approach, and then the girl did, shyly, asked in Italian what she was looking for. She pointed to the remaining earring then turned her head. "I will help," the girl said. Together they walked among the deck chairs with their heads down.

They didn't find it. The Italian girl pointed to the drain in the shower, curled her index finger to mean the size of the holes, shook her head sadly.

She waited for the distress she'd felt in school and in the cab. It didn't come. Its absence was as tangible as its presence had been. She took the remaining earring out, wrapped it in Kleenex, put it in her change purse. She spread her towel beside the Italian girl's chair, sat upright, listened to people around her speak Spanish and German and French, wondered how English sounded to somebody who didn't understand it.

The Italian girl looked puzzled, as if she wanted an explanation but didn't know how to ask for one. She cocked her head, put her hands on her hips and sighed loudly as if exasperated by the impermanence of things, of grief even. Finally she took up the search by herself, moving slowly, bent at the waist. Every few minutes she'd stop and look up, her eyes pleading: Come on, get up, look for the diamond.

# Athletes
# and
# Artists

RHEA and Charles were married on a Tuesday night. Charles' two sons and Rhea's daughter and son-in-law came to the wedding. Rhea wore a blue dress that she knew looked dated but that she'd long thought of as the absolute most beautiful dress of all times and wanted to be married in. After the ceremony, they got in two cars and drove to a small, expensive restaurant where they had rack of lamb, Rhea's favorite.

"Well, Rhea?"

"Well what?"

"Can I take pictures of you or not?"

"What is it with you and these pictures all of a sudden?"

"It's just something I want to do."

"And what about developing? Have you thought about that? Are you taking them to the drugstore? Because I'm not."

"I'll use a Polaroid. No developing."

"Did you have to ask permission? Couldn't you just have sprung it on me when I was getting out of the shower?"

"I don't want candids. I want you to pose."

"Is there something weird about this?"

"Nothing weird."

"We'll see, Charles. I guess so. We'll see."

Charles and Rhea knew one another when they were younger and married to other people. Rhea and her ex-husband and Charles and his ex-wife went to the same parties, used the same babysitters. Rhea thought Charles, the oldest member of the group and the one with the best job, was smart and serious. Charles thought Rhea danced better than any of the other women. At parties, half-drunk, he'd wait for the commotion that meant Rhea was moving the coffee table, making room for dancing.

Once, when a group of them went to the shore for the day, a woman, one of their circle, lost her bridgework in the ocean and was going to have to sit under an umbrella all day with no front teeth. She cried with her hand over her mouth while her husband yelled about four hundred dollars wasted. Rhea volunteered to drive the woman home. Charles watched their faces as they pulled out. The woman sobbing and shaking her head, Rhea looking left and right.

Twenty years later Charles saw Rhea in a department store, thought instantly of that morning on the beach, and said, "Rhea Tyrone."

"I got it," Charles said. "And three rolls of film. They're not rolls, actually. They're cartridges."

"Let's see. How much?"

"Seventy all together, on sale from a hundred and nine."

When they first talked about getting married, Charles said it would be best to sell both houses and buy a condominium. "A clean start and no hard work." The three or four places they saw looked chintzy to Rhea. "They skimped on this one, Charles," she whispered. "They skimped all over the place."

She decided they should sit down, compare both houses and move into the better of the two. They made lists. Charles had central air. Rhea had an enormous kitchen. They both had six-percent mortgages. Charles had a new driveway, concrete. Rhea had walk-in closets. Charles was in a better neighborhood, which tipped the scales. "Neighborhood is everything," the real estate agent said.

Charles, feeling a little guilty about having won the house competition, watched gratefully while Rhea sold most of his furniture.

"Do you read pornography, Charles?"

"Have you ever seen me read pornography?"

"I thought you might have started. I checked your closet for magazines."

"You didn't happen to see those grey slacks of mine while you were in there, did you?"

"The grey pants are gone. Gone. I thought we'd agreed on that."

Rhea's first marriage blew up. Her husband went to a parents' night at their daughter's school, met Terry's softspoken sixth-grade teacher, and asked for a divorce. All in a month.

After seventeen years, Charles' wife screamed and said she was getting out. Charles had stood for a moment, filled with admiration for her outburst. His own rage was so thoroughly under control.

With Rhea, he found moments when all of the vagueness fell away, moments of intense, soothing focus. They'd be in a diner, Rhea ordering, her eyes open wide, the waitress standing off to one side. He'd lean back, watch, and not know what he wanted when it was his turn.

"What about Saturday night?"

"No good. I'm having dinner with Terry."

"Sunday?"

"I can't help feeling this should be a bit more spontaneous."

"Sunday, yes or no?"

"Sunday afternoon, then. Not morning, afternoon."

The morning after the wedding, Rhea got up with Charles and made him coffee. She sat on his lap while he drank it. After he left for work, she walked around the house in bare feet, looking around corners and up at the ceilings.

For a year or so, Rhea got up, made coffee, and sat on Charles' lap or on a chair next to him. He moved quickly in his white shirt and dark tie while she sat still in her rumpled pajamas. Rhea loved her mornings, the conversation and then the quiet.

"Okay. Okay, now. Make as though you're opening the oven."

"Don't take it from behind, Charles. Take it from the front."

"I'll take it both ways."

"I'm opening the oven."

"There."

"Let me see it. Give it to me."

"It takes sixty seconds, a minute."

"Here it comes. Oh no."

"What?"

"It's bad, Charles. Look how dark."

"Turn on that light. I'll open the curtains. Okay, back by the stove. Sort of look over your shoulder."

"Like this?"

"Good. Move your — let's see — your left arm down. Look dead at me and don't smile. Look normal with your eyes."

"Take the damn picture."

"One, two . . ."

"Give it to me."

When Charles got out of bed one morning, Rhea woke up just long enough to pull her legs into the warm spot. She opened her eyes a second time when she smelled cologne.

He sat on the bed to put on his socks; she moved with the tilt of the mattress until she could feel him through the blankets. He went out of the room for what seemed like a minute or two, came back, then kissed her on the nose and mouth. She tasted coffee and toothpaste.

For Rhea, the new morning routine felt like the old one without the distractions that being fully awake had allowed. Curled in the center of that big bed, in the half-light from the bathroom, she lost the sense of the perimeters of her own body. As her own outline blurred, Charles' became sharper. He seemed even busier. His hair shined. His tie shined. She listened to him try to be quiet.

On days when she slept through the two kisses and woke with a start in the bright quiet room, she felt like a girl who has been ordered to take a nap in preparation for some late-night adult event, and does, only to wake up and think she's slept through the night and missed everything.

"Go wet your head."

"What?"

"Wet your head in the sink. Let's see how it looks."

"Okay, but then that's all."

"All right."

"This reminds me of when I was a teenager, wetting my head in the sink. I don't know why we were always doing that, washing our hair in the kitchen. Get me a towel."

"Don't dry it too much. Let's go into the living room, on the couch."

"I know, light the fire."

"By the time I do that your hair will be dry."

"You're big on this wet hair thing, aren't you?"


On the fourth Saturday of every month, Rhea had lunch or dinner with her daughter. Each drove fifty miles to meet the other. It was Terry, not Rhea, who insisted on the strict once-a-month schedule.

"I'm tired of salad bars," Rhea said. "The whole point of going out to lunch is to have somebody else bring the food to you."

"Come on. It's supposed to be great."

Terry took two glass plates out of a cooler and handed one to her mother, who was standing on her tiptoes, trying to get a look at the food.

"Don't put too much lettuce on your plate. You won't have room for anything substantial. I hate salad bars, but I understand them," Rhea said, watching what other people put on their plates. Her eyes moved from the spoon or tongs to the hand, up the arm to the face. At the bread board, she cut enough bread for everyone.

"Mom," Terry said.

"I couldn't help it. It was one of those things like when you get stuck holding the door. The blonde fellow thinks I work here. Did you hear him? 'Sourdough, please.' "

As they sat down, Terry said, "How's Charles?"

"Fine, I think."

"You think?"

"He wants to take pictures of me without my clothes on."

"You're kidding."

"Don't laugh."

"I can't help it."

"Nothing dirty, you understand. Just these sort of around the house things."

"It's kind of touching, actually."

"You think?"

"Well, yeah. I mean, he adores you."

"Mmmm," Rhea said and took a long drink of water.

"If it bothers you, the pictures, don't do it."

"It's not that it bothers me so much as that I just don't understand."

"Come on. It's not exactly whips and chains. You're flattered by it, I can tell."

"No. I was sort of flattered at first. I thought it would be sexy and all. But it's not. I get the feeling it isn't working. He isn't getting what he wanted out of it."

"You're doing it already? I thought we were still at the discussion stage here."

"We have almost a hundred pictures."

"And why does he say he wants to take them?"

"He says it's just something he wants to do, which would be fine. Except he gets this look in his eyes when we're taking them. Like he's trying so hard. You know what it reminds me of? It drove me crazy for a week, but I finally thought of it. It reminds me of the look some of the Olympic athletes had in their eyes when they were interviewed after their events. Didn't matter if they'd won or lost. Like if they'd jumped twenty feet, they needed to jump thirty."

Alone in the car on the way home, Rhea repeated bits of what she'd said to Terry at the restaurant. She took one hand off the steering wheel and gestured with it, palm up, while she talked.

When she got home, Charles was sitting at the kitchen table, the stack of photographs in front of him.

"What were you doing just now? What were you thinking about while you looked at them?"

"How was lunch?"

"Don't ignore the question and don't think. Just answer."

"Rhea, we've been through this."

"We have not. You're not telling me the truth."

"You're upset. We won't take anymore. Forget it."

"I am upset. I'm upset and don't tell me to forget it."

She picked up the first picture in the stack, looked at it closely, then held it against the second.

"You're a smart man, Charles. You don't do something as outrageous as this without having some sense of why you're doing it. Now come on."

"Come on what? Rhea, you're beautiful. If I were a painter and wanted to do you in the nude, you'd be thrilled. It's as simple as that. Not everything in the world is complicated."

Charles sat alone in the living room, his arms extended out in front of him, a photograph in each hand. He thought of Rhea as she'd been when she'd come home that afternoon — she'd tried to get him to look her in the eye and her hand had tilted so far it had almost touched her shoulder — and looked at a shot of her standing in front of the refrigerator.

He listened to her get out of bed, walk down the hall, come into the room, and sit down beside him.

"The pictures again, huh?"

Charles rubbed his face with the tips of his fingers, pulling the skin down then pushing it up.

"Just explain to me what it's about."

He looked at her for a moment then said, "Sometimes when I look at you . . . I get such a sense of a picture. Everything is just right, the colors, the lines, the proportions. I wanted to get that, to capture it, to bring it through me and say here it is. But it didn't work. The way you think a painter must paint a picture, a beautiful picture, and everybody loves it and he knows he's failed. Except for may be a crease in the wrist or something he wasn't able to get whatever it was — the particular beauty of the thing — that made him want to paint it in the first place."

Rhea put her slippered feet on the coffee table and stared at the space between them. "Keep talking."

"I don't know how else to explain it."

"Don't try to explain. Just talk about it."

Charles spread his fingers and looked at his open palms.

"Sometimes with you there are moments when about twenty thousand things chink into place, things that the rest of the time are just slightly off. There's a kind of hum to it. I can just take it in without knowing, while it's happening, what's so wonderful about it."

Rhea rocked the upper part of her body in a kind of nod and said, "Remember when we were first married we'd get up together in the morning and have coffee? Then I stopped getting up. I lost the one dose of you sitting next to me, but I got you moving around in the dark. It's better because I'm doing even less to get it. That's something like what you're talking about, isn't it?"

Charles smiled and nodded. "Let's have a drink."

They went into the kitchen where they stood at the counter and drank wine, leaning into each other. Rhea rubbed her forehead against Charles' chest.

When their glasses were empty, they separated and went around the kitchen and living room, turning off lights. As she walked behind him down the hall, Rhea put her hands on Charles' shoulders.

# Teeth and
# Nails

A YOUNG woman walked past Mike and his father, dropped a faded cloth pocketbook on the counter, and said, "Can you tell me what you do with the dead cats?"

"I beg your pardon?" the man behind the counter said.

Mike and his father waited to see if she'd say it again.

"The cats. I know this sounds real bizarre, but it's not. I'm a taxidermist and I want to do a cat. Can I buy a dead one?"

"I don't know. Nobody ever asked before. Let me check with my supervisor."

Looking at the back of the woman's head, Mike's father said, "If you want a dog, why don't you spend a couple of bucks and get something decent? Anything you get here's guaranteed full of worms."

The woman put her hand to her mouth and called, "Excuse me. Before you go can you tell me if the bodies are in good shape?"

"They're fine, perfect. We kill by injection. I'll just be a minute."

Mike said, "I got Tony here, Dad, and he's fine."

"Tony. Jesus, I hate it when people name dogs people names. Can you tell me what you did when you had somebody over the house named Tony? You walk into a guy's house and his dog has the same name as you."

"The kids named him."

The woman turned around, smiled at Mike, and said, "I want a dead cat."

Mike's father leaned in to get a look at her face. "Yeah?" he said. "Terrific. We want a live dog. Come on, Mike. Let's see what's here."

"What do you want with a dead cat?" Mike said.

His father headed off towards the row of turquoise cages.

"I'm a taxidermist. Well, actually I'm a jeweler, but I'm getting into taxidermy. I love cats. They're so independent. I'd love to do one. What do you do?"

"I'm unemployed since May. You need a practice cat, then?"

"Exactly. I just finished my first squirrel. He's a composite made from three different squirrels, all hit by cars. I never kill anything or anything. Was that your father?"

Mike nodded. "He thinks if he's not here to supervise I'll bring home a Great Dane."

"You live with him?"

"For now."

"For now?"

"I just separated from my wife."

The man behind the counter said, "Okay. She's not sure but she thinks there might be a health regulation forbidding the sale of dead animals. God knows we could use the money. Anyway, she said you should check back in a couple of days."

"Thank you. I will." The woman picked up her pocket-book, leaned back against the counter, and said, "What did you do before you were unemployed?"

"Taught college. American history."

"Really? I always liked history, especially the Civil War."

"My specialty."

"Why'd you stop?"

"I was fired."

"Oh. Sorry."

"No."

"You didn't like it?"

"Teaching was all right, but I used to sit in my office and imagine I could hear the administration digging tunnels under my chair. It was a relief when the floor finally gave way."

"Like gophers, huh?"

"More like cave miners. Do you want to go with me tonight?"

"I'd like to, but I can't. I'm giving this party. Why don't you come?"


The door was opened by a fat middle-aged woman who was on the phone. "Come on in," she said, the receiver on her shoulder. "You must be Mike. I'm Emily. Janey should be right down." She took the telephone into a brightly lit bathroom and closed the door.

There were platters of hors d'oeuvres on the counters and table. On a shelf above the sink there was a small stuffed lizard. Its eyes had been replaced by red stones.

A triangular piece of hammered gold stuck out of its open mouth.

"The first piece I ever finished," Janey said. "A former pet." She was wearing a white cotton dress and looked prettier in the kitchen than she had in the pound. "Did you find the house okay?"

"No problem. I used to live around here."

Mike handed her the two pounds of apricots he'd decided on over Mexican beer. They were ripe, out-of-season, and expensive.

"These are beautiful," she said, peering into the bag. "They remind me of cheeks," She put a handful in the middle of a plate of soft cheeses that was on the table.

"Have you lived here long?"

"About three years. It's Emily's house. You met Emily, right?" Janey said looking around.

"She's in there," Mike said, looking toward the closed bathroom door. "You're roommates?"

"We live together, but we're not roommates."

"Oh," Mike said, nodding. "What are you?"

"Emily and I have been together for a long time, forever. I got out with men too, though. I always have," Janey said.

"You should have told me at the pound."

"No. You wouldn't have come."

The bathroom door opened.

"Don't look so guilty, Mike," Emily said. "You want a beer?"

She took two bottles of dark beer out of the refrigerator and motioned for Mike to sit down. Janey went to the counter and began arranging pieces of raw broccoli and cauliflower on a silver tray. Mike watched her for a moment, trying to detect signs of awkwardness in her movements. There were none. She might have been alone as she alternated the green and white vegetables.

"Janey said you teach American history?"

"Taught American history. I lost my job in May."

Emily ran her thumbnail through the label on her beer bottle.

Janey carried the finished platter and a bowl of beige dip into the living room.

"Put ashtrays around in there," Emily called after her, then put her hand on Mike's forearm.

"No sense being angry. I see you looking at her like you expect her to be worried about it. Forget it. Janey doesn't give a damn about other people. I don't mean that exactly. She just sort of drifts through her day, bumping into people and smiling. Ask her and she'll tell you she has all these emotional needs that can't be met by any one person. Bullshit. It's a response she's figured out over the years and likes." Emily gestured toward the living room with her thumb and said, "She has no needs."

Mike put his beer bottle to his lips and swallowed several times. He felt as though he should wonder why Emily was telling him all of this. But he didn't wonder at all. He just wanted to hear whatever she had to say.

"I love her so I put up with it."

The doorbell rang and Emily got up to answer it.

By eleven o'clock there were about forty people at the party. Mike sat in the kitchen talking to a woman in her fifties who was a law student, but he kept his eye on Janey. Her white dress made her easy to spot. He watched her kiss a bald man on the lips. She sent a teenaged boy to the store for more ice. While the law student described the way professional ethics were taught, Janey was persuaded to jitterbug. When he lost sight of her, he excused himself to go look for her.

He found her sitting alone on the stairs.

"Come on," she said. "I want to show you my studio."

He followed her up the stairs, his eyes on the slope of her rear end. At the end of the hall, she opened the door to what should have been the master bedroom.

It smelled like a high school biology lab. Sheets with a faded floral print covered most of the floor. Spools of plastic thread the size of peanut butter jars stood on a plywood workbench under a bright light.

Janey picked up a stuffed squirrel that was curled like a sleeping cat.

"This is my squirrel."

"I never saw one asleep."

"I know. Neither did I. That's why I need the cat. If I get one, I'll position her like this and put her on the rocking chair downstairs. You just can't get the same effect with a squirrel."

In the strong light, Mike was able to see a faint scar below Janey's nose that distorted the outline of her lip.

"Feel how heavy he is." She handed him the squirrel. He leaned back, not wanting to touch it. It fell to the floor.

"I'm sorry," Mike said, kneeling slowly to pick it up.

Janey leaned over and kissed him on the mouth. As

he straightened up, he wanted to pull her close, but the squirrel — its weight distracting in his hand — was between them. As much as the kiss was hindered by the squirrel, it was helped by Janey's being taller than Mike's wife: his neck was bent at a pleasantly unfamiliar angle.

Janey turned her head, abruptly ending the kiss. She walked over to a tall stool, the only one in the room, and sat down. Mike put the squirrel down on the workbench.

"You having a good time at the party?"

"Fine. I was talking to that woman who's in law school, Mary somebody."

"She's Emily's friend. Emily's a new lawyer."

"I like her, Emily, but I can't help feeling a little sorry for her."

"Feeling sorry? Emily doesn't need you feeling sorry for her."

"No, I know."

"I hate that. Feeling sorry. People think they're doing you a big favor. But in order to feel sorry for somebody, you first have to think, God, I wouldn't be in his shoes for anything."

Mike walked over to Janey and took her hand. He was about to kiss her again when she said, "Would you mind going downstairs? I feel like working. I'll be down in a while."

Mike stepped back and dropped Janey's hand. His eyes had been closed, moving in for the kiss, and he knew Janey had seen that. "Oh. Oh, okay. I guess I'll see you in a little while, then."

On his way down the stairs, Mike missed a step and

arrived in the living room squatting, one leg tucked under, the other sticking straight out in front.

He recovered in a single movement and walked to the picnic table bar, which was again without ice. Two women came over to check on his condition; they thought he was drunk. He told them he was fine, poured scotch into a wine glass, and drank it in one swallow.

He closed his eyes and was glad Janey hadn't seen him fall. He knew she had dismissed him. He felt flushed and a little sick. He didn't know what he was supposed to have done up there. Whatever it was, he thought, must have been something pretty damn exciting. He thought of her sitting cross-legged on the floor of her studio, examining some bit of fur.

He chased the scotch with water scooped out of the penguin-shaped ice bucket and decided to leave. On his way through the empty kitchen, he stopped and slipped the stuffed lizard into his jacket pocket.

He drove to his wife's house. It looked secure, dark and closed, except that one trash can was lying on its side, wet garbage spilling out of the torn plastic bag.

With habitual irritation, he got out of the car, walked to the curb, and carefully uprighted the can. He stooped to pick up a steak bone that had escaped, then wiped his hands on the damp grass. Satisfied, he got back in his car which he'd left running with the defrost on full. The dry heat made him squint.

He parked on the street in front of his father's house. As he went up the stairs, he felt how well his body knew the rhythm of the climb. He knew just where to put his foot on each step in anticipation of the next.

The kitchen light was on. His father had trouble sleeping through the night and would often, after a few hours in bed, sit drinking tea until morning.

"Hey,"

"You home?"

"I'm home."

"Do the chain. I got in bed and couldn't remember if I'd put the chain up or not. I had to get up and check. Sure enough, I'd locked you out."

"Where's Chester?"

"I never saw anything like it. You'd think he lived here all his life. He ate two cans of food, walked around a little, not too much, then planted himself on the rug in the parlor. Dead asleep since ten o'clock. That's one old dog. He's no seven or eight like that guy told us. No sir. I can tell by the way when he looks at you he only turns his head instead of his whole body. His drooping head just swings to one side. Did you have a good time?"

"Okay. Broke up kind of early though."

"What early? It's after one."

Mike looked at the kitchen curtains and wondered if they'd been washed since his mother had died. They were dingy white and sheer and made him think of nurses' stockings.

He took the lizard out of his pocket and stood it up on his open palm under the table.

"I'm going out tomorrow and buy myself a pair of shoes," his father said. "All my heels are worn down. I think that's what's making my back hurt. I read about it. You want to come and get yourself a pair?"

"No thanks, Dad. I don't need shoes."

Mike pressed his thumbnail into the seam that ran along the lizard's belly, remembering the plastic thread.

"I was glad to see you get out tonight. It's no good, you spending so much time in that room."

Mike balanced the lizard on his knee, then looked up and saw Chester standing in the doorway.

"Hey, com'ere Chester, you old shit," Mike said. "What do you think, huh? What do you think?" He ran his hands over the dog's face and down into the fur between its front legs. The lizard dropped from his knee to the floor. He scratched Chester's back and wrapped one hand around his tail. "I think we have to call you Old Chester. Old Chesterfield."

"You going out with her again?"

"Nah. She's too young."

Chester slipped under the table, lizard in mouth.

"At least you got out."

# Breakfast,
# Lunch, and
# Dinner

Food was there at the start. We met when he asked me to pass him a basket of cheddar cheese Goldfish. I was happy to do it because before he'd sat down I'd had those fish all to myself and had fallen into a rhythm of taking a sip, eating a fish, taking a sip, etc. I didn't want to give them up altogether, though, so I slid the basket along the bar until it was equidistant between us. He took a handful and said he hadn't had any dinner. I smiled and nodded as if to say I know what that's like, even though I didn't and don't. He put a couple of fish in his mouth, then shook the ones left in his fist like they were dice he was getting ready to throw.

After more nods and smiles from me and more fish rattling from him, he turned to get the bartender's attention. I selected a fish from the basket. Before I was able to put it in my mouth, he asked if he could buy me a drink. I said yes, using the hand that held the fish between thumb and index finger to gesture. I don't remember why a simple yes needed gestures — I was either thanking him excessively or taking a roundabout route to yes by way of no. I didn't put that fish in my mouth until he turned to pay for the drinks.

Our conversation moved by fits and starts through the better part of an hour. When I got up to leave he asked if

I would meet him there the following night. I said I would and did. That second night, as it came to be known, we stayed until closing time then went to a diner where he ordered sausage and eggs, so I did too. He had his eggs up. I had mine scrambled. I didn't think I could handle all of that gooey yolk attractively.

He drove me back to my car and we kissed for a good long time in the parking lot. It was winter and there was a lot of wool coat between us. Driving home, I sat up straight and wished there were more cars on the road. I felt alert and out-going. Driving, especially on the deserted road, didn't seem like enough to be doing.

He called me early the next morning and said he was tired but happy and asked me to dinner. In the restaurant, rubbing my knuckles with his thumbs, he said, "I don't want to scare you, but I think I'm falling in love." I said I thought I was too. That's when I started to cook.

I was unemployed so my days were spent getting ready. Like a European, I'd go to a butcher for meat, a fishstore for seafood, a vegetable market for produce, a bakery for bread, and — very important, we were new and nervous — to a liquor store for wine. I'd get back to my apartment around noon, deposit the various paper bags on the counter, then stand in front of the refrigerator and eat a half a tomato as if it was a cupcake, biting around the edges then popping the center in my mouth whole. I was too giddy to want to eat, and too concerned with how my stomach would look later in bed, but I didn't want hunger pangs interfering with my ability to concentrate on my cooking.

The recipes I was going to use had, of course, already been selected from the fat *Joy of Cooking*. I'd read through them to determine what needed to be done first. Veal might have to be submerged in marinade or chicken rinsed in cool water and set, uncovered, on a plate in the refrigerator. If I was making Caesar salad — he loved it and would eat even the soggiest leaves — olive oil (*none other*, the book warned) had to be poured into a glass jar with a clove of garlic. The jar had to be covered and set in the sun on the kitchen window sill. Several times during an afternoon, I'd pick up that jar, turn it over in my hands, and watch the garlic move through the oil.

I'd do everything I could except set the table — there is something sad about a table set for dinner at one-thirty in the afternoon — then go and take a long shower. I'd rinse determinedly until the hot water gave out because I'd read enough women's magazines to know the importance of rinsing. (Vidal Sassoon thinks you should rinse your hair until your arms ache. I think I was about ten when I read that interview.) When the water was colder than I could stand, I'd step out, wrap my head in a towel, then rub the bargain body lotion I was buying to counterbalance the expensive groceries, into my skin. Still moist in creases, I'd dress carefully but casually — I didn't want to look *dressed* — then it was back to the kitchen to turn the oil-and-garlic jar and wait until I could start cooking.

By the time I'd hear his car, everything would be just on the verge of readiness. I'd go and stand at the top of the stairs. As he'd make his way up we'd smile at one another, a little embarrassed but also genuinely relieved to be together again, as though each of us was afraid that the other had had a change of heart during the course of the day and decided to call the whole thing off.

As he'd pull me close I'd be aware of things bubbling and needing basting behind me. He'd sit down at the table. I'd show off at the stove. The final stages were flashy. I knew I looked like an expert, doing several things at once, all of them aromatic.

He'd pause after nearly every mouthful to tell me things were delicious. He'd have seconds, sometimes thirds. I'd been intensely involved with that food all day — inspecting, selecting, paying, washing, tossing, sautéing, serving — and was tired of it. With him there, handsome and husband-like in front of me, it couldn't get my attention. Anyway, not eating meant more prominent hipbones for later.

As the weeks passed it got easier to be with him. We moved through our meals with just the sounds of forks against plates and wine into glasses. Touching him, a finger on his forearm, a foot on his chair, seemed to complete the sensation of good food in my mouth.

No longer cooking with win-or-lose urgency, I was less familiar with the food by the time it made the table. I ate as much as he did. My stomach wasn't a factor any longer. However it was would be fine.

We went to restaurants a couple of times a week and ordered with complete abandon. We had appetizers, bottles of wine, and when the dinner plates were cleared, we had Grand Marnier with our coffee. There was an unspoken financial agreement: I bought the fixings for elaborate dinners and he picked up eighty-five-dollar checks.

We took the security we'd found at the table with us when we got up. After lunch one Saturday, we went shopping for a pair of shoes together. Looking in the store window, I leaned back and felt his belly in the small of my back. In a fit of contentment, he bought a pair of black shoes he was never going to put on without first saying he didn't know why he'd bought them. I'd see him reach for them and wait for him to say what he always said, "I hate these shoes."

Gradually I stopped using serving dishes. Food went from the pan to the plates. With an eye on my grocery bill, I cut out the wine. We drank iced tea or water. I no longer needed recipes. I knew about how long it took to cook a chicken or a chop and was confident enough to experiment with seasonings.

I began having to send him to the store for things I'd forgotten. He spent twenty minutes walking up and down supermarket aisles looking for capers. "Are they fish or vegetables or what?" he snapped when he got back.

By then he'd all but officially moved in. One morning we were up and getting dressed, not realizing the severity of the snowstorm outside, when his boss called and told him not to bother coming in, the roads were a mess. My mother was next. "You're not even thinking about driving are you?" I waited for my boss to call — I'd gotten a job answering the telephone in a doctor's office — but he didn't. I left a message on his answering machine.

We got undressed and took our coffee back to bed with

us. We thought we'd spend the whole day there, but in an hour we were up and hungry. We put on all the snow clothes we could find and walked the six blocks to the A & P. We bought eggs, cheese, English muffins, Canadian bacon, and a coffee cake. On the way home we passed one of those square trucks that deliver potato chips to people's houses. It was stuck in a driveway. He wanted to ask the driver if we could buy a tin of chips. "No," I said. "Come on. We have enough."

He spread a blanket on the living room floor while I went to work in the kitchen. We turned on HBO, ate, snoozed, fooled around, and watched movies all day and into the night. At three o'clock in the morning we were wide awake watching a movie about a couple who did nothing but go for walks and talk. These two walked through endless parks and down city streets. They walked alongside rivers that blurred and became crowded outdoor markets. Most of their conversations were about dreams one or the other had had, long dreams that sounded like they were being made up on the spot. When I found myself waiting for the "and thens" — "And then, suddenly I was in hell . . . and then a girl I secretly loved in high school was there . . . and then I knew they were going to bury me alive" — I got up and turned it off. We crawled into bed to sleep some more.

When the alarm went off the next morning, I was already in the shower. He opened the bathroom door and asked me to please hurry up. I stayed in longer than I would have if he hadn't emphasized the please, then went into the kitchen to make coffee.

There were dishes in the sink and on the counters. The spatula was face down in the frying pan, bits of cheese on its edges. The milk had been left out and smelled sour, which put an end to the coffee since neither of us would drink it black.

In the living room, the blanket was still on the floor and the television was not in its usual spot. I didn't touch anything, didn't even throw out the sour milk.

When I went back into the bedroom, he was pulling on his pants. As I buttoned my skirt, I had the sense that we were competing to see which of us could get out into the white responsible world first.

He stopped volunteering to go to the supermarket without me. The tomatoes he'd brought back were always too soft, the pork chops too thick, anyway. We started food shopping together. My spirits would lift as we'd pull into the parking lot. I'd get to buy things I wouldn't have if he wasn't there to pay the bill. Like artichokes. Yogurt-covered peanuts. Spring water. He'd push the cart and I'd dart off and back again. When it took me a while to decide on something, he'd catch up to me. I'd know he was behind me because he'd tap me softly on the rear end with the cart.

Since he was paying for the groceries, dinners out became something I had to press to get. I knew as I opened the menu, large and leatherette, how to make trouble if I wanted to.

Towards the end of one scratchy Saturday afternoon, I gave him an ultimatum. "I want to go out," I said. We went to a gaudy twenty-fifth-anniversary kind of place where I, pushing hard, had ordered a second bottle of wine by the time a white-haired lady came to the table and asked if we'd like to have our picture taken. When he said no I said yes. She took it, six dollars was added to our bill, and he was furious.

I found his tight-fistedness so unattractive. The financial finagling that I was doing, the transfer of the grocery bill from me to him that I'd engineered, seemed somehow feminine and so my birthright.

A week later I got the picture in the mail. Our faces look fleshy and fixed, his in anger, mine in drunken I-dare-you.

We began to take food with us in the car. Like an alcoholic husband and wife with their mayonnaise jar of gin, we had our hard pretzels and Kit Kat bars.

We were getting ready to drive to the shore for the day — the shore meant sausage and peppers, clams on the half shell. He was sitting out in the car waiting for me. I was on my way out the door when I realized we had no food for the way down. Nothing. I was in the kitchen putting pears in a plastic bag when I heard the car horn. I went to the window and looked out. He saw me and changed from one long blast to a series of short toots. I stood and listened. He leaned out of the car and shouted, "What's taking you?"

"Snacks," I shrieked back, stretching out the middle of the word so that it lasted for several seconds.

The end came when he had the courage to say out loud

that all we shared was appetite. I knew he was right, had even tried to justify the situation to myself — other couples had the opera or the New York Mets — and failed. But there in the serious afternoon light, it was too humiliating to admit.

I tried to dislodge food from its spot at the top of our agenda. I checked the "What's Happening" column in Friday's paper. On Saturday morning I asked, "What do you want to do today?" as though we generally did things. I'd already chosen an antique auction, though neither one of us knew anything about old furniture beyond that we liked it in a vague sort of way.

He agreed to go immediately and said seventy miles wasn't too far to drive. There was a lot of chirpy conversation in the car. We commented on things as we passed them, deer and factory outlets.

After two sets of directions from pedestrians, we pulled up to a field that had rows of folding chairs on it. There were clusters of people in the first couple of rows only.

"Hasn't it started yet?" I asked one of two young men who were loading a bedroom set onto the back of a pick up.

"You kidding?" he said, slamming the gate of his truck closed. "It's in full swing."

The other guy seemed to understand how important the auction was to me and said, "Most of the dealers stayed away. The organizers are demanding a too-high percentage."

We stayed for a little while, sitting side-by-side in the otherwise empty fifth row.

On the way home we stopped and bought a pizza with extra cheese and mushrooms. I insisted on setting out plates and napkins before we opened the box.

We each had one piece pretty happily, but halfway through the second I was trying not to cry and having trouble swallowing. There seemed to be dry space in my mouth around the bite of pizza.

He looked at me then stood up. He tipped his plate over the garbage pail, put it in the sink, and said, "I'm going, okay? I'll call you." I nodded and kept nodding while I listened to him go down the stairs.

# Scrawl

SOMEBODY has spray-painted *EARL M. MUD SUCKING PIG IS DEAD* on the side of my house. Day-Glo pink, letters a foot high.

I walk toward it, hear myself say Jesus, rush to the street and look one way and then the other as if I expect to see whoever did it running. From the curb I turn and stare. My hands untie and retie the sash of my robe.

A strange sense of humiliation settles over me. I realize I'd been feeling good, even hopeful. The first cool morning after a week of heat and dense clouds. Joyce and I had slept heavily. The drone of the air conditioner made our bedroom feel like an isolation chamber. Her hand was on my chest when I opened my eyes. And now this. The paint has run, making the whole thing look vaguely like a Halloween decoration.

Earl's lying on the floor in the family room eating cereal out of the box. He doesn't acknowledge me, gazes steadily at the TV. There's something distinctly animal about him when he's up negotiating the house for himself, when I come upon him stirring chocolate syrup into his milk or standing on a chair to reach the doughnuts on top of the refrigerator. He's all instinct, zero self-awareness, like a dog you don't know walking on your lawn.

Joyce is sprawled across the center of our bed. I put my hand on her shoulder and she bolts upright, kicks the sheets off, lunges out of bed. Why does she always have to get up this way? You wouldn't expect it from somebody who loves to sleep, somebody who walks around half the day in a snit if I wake her before noon on weekends. You'd think she'd lie there blinking for a time then sit on the edge of the bed, head down, arms straight. Not Joyce. She barrels out of bed.

We go and stand on the lawn, the three of us. "Oh, Earl," Joyce says angrily. "What is this?"

Earl seems to be sounding out the words, but he can't be, can he? Surely a sentence like this gets taken in whole no matter how poorly a kid reads. It strikes me that it is a sentence, not just an epithet. The side of the house speaks to us.

"Have you any idea who would do this?" I say in a voice that is stern though I hadn't meant it to be.

Earl glares at me, his eyes so expressive I read them like words: Don't hurt me now.

"Earl?" Joyce says tenderly.

At the sound of her voice he takes off, runs into the neighbor's yard then cuts back into ours. He's out of sight now but we can hear him crying. Joyce and I don't look at each other or at the side of the house.

"Let *me* go after him," she says finally.

Joyce brings Earl inside, pulls him onto her lap, presses his head to her chest, murmurs to him until he reluctantly names a suspect. I get right on the phone with the mother who shouts at me. I'd hoped we'd form a coalition of concerned parents, teach our children that it is better to be nice. Instead this ignorant woman, her voice gravelly and harsh, tells me I'd better have proof before I accuse her son. "You didn't see him do it, you can go to hell."

Joyce looks at me while she comforts Earl. Her expression says well, *well?* I retreat into the kitchen. She follows right on my heels and I wonder how brusquely Earl was cleared from her lap. We stand by the sink and something despicable happens. We look in each other's eyes and for one second we're on the side of the spray-painter. We're ashamed to be the parents of an unpopular boy.

I get away from her, go back to the family room where Earl is sitting two feet from the television. There's no trace of the animal left. He's human now. I ask him what kind of boy this Stanley Haiduk is. Much bigger than you? Has he given you trouble before? Stanley is big, Earl says, big and fat. He's shoved Earl against the bulletin board, knocked his books out of his arms. Stanley chants Mary, Mary, Mary when Earl goes by.

"Mary?"

"Mary means gay."

Perfectly deadpan. The spray-painting has exposed Earl so completely he doesn't care what I know now.


JOYCE was my secretary. My first wife had been dead for three years. I worked long hours, occasionally had dinner out with business associates, watched ball games in a neighborhood bar. I didn't consider myself lonely. It seemed I had geared down to accommodate what my life had become. Joyce pursued me, asked for rides home, suggested we stop for drinks. In the office she made me out to be a stodgy old guy while she played the ditzy blonde.

I was flattered. Here was a young woman willing to sleep with me. More than willing. She'd run her hand up my thigh while I drove, would lick and nip and suck on my thumb to show me what was going to happen later. I spent a dozen or so glorious nights in her small apartment and then she told me she was pregnant, tearfully, said she wouldn't consider abortion. Either I married her or she'd put the baby up for adoption. I told her I needed a few days to think and she nodded solemnly. I told myself it was time I remarried, and why not a younger woman? Elena's death had receded in my consciousness. I was not the man I'd been before it happened, but I wasn't actively suffering anymore. Compared to the passion and raucousness of sleeping with Joyce, the way I'd been living seemed colorless. I'd been moving in a netherworld, I decided, convinced myself that Joyce had come—been sent?— to bring me back to Earth. And I was secretly proud of impregnating this youngish woman who did aerobics on her lunch hour and read *Cosmopolitan* magazine.

Beware setting out to start a new life. Joyce and I are as incompatible as two people can be. She is shallow and mean-spirited; what was erotic has become crude. She thinks I am pretentious and dull, not much of a man. I know she is biding her time, gearing up to leave me. When she does, I'll go back to the life I was leading after Elena because that is my true life. Only one thing will be different. I have a son now, a flesh and blood child. Earl's existence is as solid to me as Elena's death.

I WANT to paint over the scrawl before lunch but Joyce insists I go to the police station and file a report. I take Earl with me. In the car he is sullen. What I see when I look over at him is the nape of his neck twisted away from me. The cop is patronizing and I curse Joyce for sending us. He makes me dictate the sentence then looks right at Earl. Earl's eyes dart around in their sockets.

Goddamn it if we don't get home and find Joyce sound asleep on the couch. What kind of mother is able to sleep inside a house defaced in the way ours has been? Twice in one day I have to watch her wake up. She pounces on Earl as if he brings news, then tells me to go see this Haiduk woman. "Let her know we mean business."

EARL was named for my father-in-law, Joyce's smarmy attempt to get back in the old man's good graces after she'd defied him by marrying me. He said I was too old, shouted age ratios like word problems at her over the telephone so loudly I could hear his voice from across the room. "When you're forty, he'll be sixty-four. You'll wind up being his nurse."

The delivery room brutalized me. I had never witnessed anybody in that kind of pain. As will always happen when I am faced with a thing enormous and hard, when circumstances are as extreme as they get, I felt Elena with me. It was as if she and I were watching this girl scream and bleed. When they put the baby on Joyce's bare breasts and she told me she wanted to name him Earl, I agreed instantly.

THE Haiduk house smells like a wet dog. Mrs. Haiduk looks too old to be the mother of a third grader and I feel a kinship with her. Four teenaged girls are lounging on the couch and floor, all barely dressed. Short shorts and bathing suit tops, T-shirts and underwear. My eyes pass over a thigh, a flat flat stomach and I wonder if one of the girls is Stanley's real mother.

"I talked to my boy about all this," Mrs. Haiduk says in a conciliatory tone I didn't expect. Perhaps she's glad I'm old too. "From what he tells me there's any number of kids could have done it. It's a lousy thing and I'm sorry for your Earl."

I can't bear Mrs. Haiduk's sympathy in front of her blank-eyed daughters. "May I speak to Stanley?" I ask, enunciating for all I'm worth, sounding, suddenly, British.

"Suit yourself. He's out back playing."

Stanley is a big kid in a tight black T-shirt. The laces of his sneakers are untied and saliva bubbles around his gums. He looks at me, sniffs hard, swallows with gusto.

"I'm Earl's father. Did you spray-paint my house last night?"

"Lots of people hate Earl," he says. "You can't prove nothing."

He's standing beside a sandbox that looks as if it hasn't been used in years. The sand is blackish and wet. I'd like to shove him down into it. "Let me see your hands," I say. He smirks, extends them. They're clean, a little raw around the cuticles. The nails are bleached white.

"If you go near Earl again, I'll beat the daylights out of you. No cops, no mothers. Just me, Stanley. I'll take you apart."

He sizes me up, takes a step back.

As I walk to my car, he snorts mightily and spits.

On the way home I think of Earl leaving for school in the morning and coming home in the afternoon after God knows what kind of horrible day. Something surges inside me. He is, after all, mine to protect.

I MAY have adjusted too well to Elena's existing only in my mind. The dead offer no resistance. They are what you want them to be when you want them to be it. There only when you conjure them up, absolutely not there otherwise. They will listen to you forever. I'm not sure I'd know what to say to Elena anymore if she weren't dead.

JOYCE has made up her mind. The entire house will have to be painted. If we do just the one side, the rest will look that much worse. She's right, but I am astonished to discover she thinks I'm going to do the job myself. Am I some young husband who strides in from work, changes into blue jeans, gets a couple of buddies to give him a hand? I tell her she'd better look in the yellow pages; she turns away disdainfully. Earl is calmer for having spent time alone with her. He stands at the stove, spatula in hand, watching over the grilled cheese sandwiches we're having for lunch.

IN bed I reach for Joyce, wanting her badly the way you want to get drunk after you've been fired. She's stingy at first, disappointed in my handling of the day's crisis, but soon enough she feels my urgency and won't waste it.

I SIT in my office and ask myself how my father would have handled this. He was an ineffectual man, for the most part, an accommodating man. He would, however, have painted over the scrawl by now, that much I know. But he wouldn't have threatened Stanley the way I did. He would have scolded him. Stanley would have had a field day with my father.

In grade school I was in chorus. The music teacher had been on Broadway or in vaudeville or some damn thing. One spring she made us do this ridiculous dance with bamboo poles. Two kids kneeled on the floor clapping these poles together while the rest of us had to take turns hopping in between them, like jumping rope. I'd gotten a couple of whacks on the ankle during rehearsals and was afraid of those poles in exactly the way I was afraid of a baseball coming right at me to catch.

The night of the spring concert, the teacher pushed me from behind when it was my turn and I lurched into the light. I was unable to move for a few seconds. Then I bolted forward and hopped into the clapping poles where my feet got away from me altogether. The girls working the poles had to set them down to let me out. My father sat in the second row smiling wanly.

Punch and cookies in the gym afterwards. My father milled around awkwardly, increasing my humiliation in ways only I knew. I ordered him to wait by the door while I went to retrieve my coat. I passed a group of older boys and they recognized me. One boy mussed my hair in what could have been good-natured horsing around and then four of them were on me, slapping and pulling at my clothes and one of them spit. My father—he'd come after me—shouted at them to leave me alone, his voice high-pitched and thin. He seemed intimidated by them, as if he wanted them to like him. He called them fellas.

WHEN I get home I make a pitcher of Rob Roys and offer Joyce one. She grimaces, so I sit on the front steps and drink alone. One and then another, half of a third. I'm drunk and glad to be when I go upstairs to put on painting clothes.

The pink blends instantly. Soon I'm contentedly running my brush over a rose-colored patch, 10' x 10', as if that's what I'd set out to do. The words are still visible but this doesn't bother me in the slightest, I've so completely lost sight of my objective. Joyce comes to the side door, shakes her head, tells me I was supposed to use a primer first. "You can't cover bright pink with one coat of white," she says, slowly, as if she's talking to a child. I stir my paint, wet my brush. The next time I look over she's gone.

I should have gone inside an hour ago but the night is cool and I've got all this paint. In the garage I find an oil lamp someone gave us, Elena and me, years ago. It glows softly, just enough light to work by. My drink is warm now, watered Scotch; the taste lingers in my mouth. I leave white fingerprints on the glass.

I am the only thing moving in the neighborhood now. One by one the lights in my house go out. The air conditioner in our bedroom goes on. It's too dark to paint anymore. I sit on the grass by the lamp, feel the heat it throws, smell the smoke.

Stanley will strike again, I'm sure of it. This time I'll catch him. I'll hear footsteps on the lawn or the hiss of a spray can and I'll race downstairs and out the front door. Stanley will take off and I'll chase him, running hard in bare feet. The sharp stones and rough pavement will urge me on. When I'm close enough, when I can hear him panting, I'll get him, grab hold of his T-shirt and yank with all my might. What I'll do then, Elena, I can't say. You may know. You probably do.

# Morpheus

ADRIEN is here with me now, down on one knee, folding laundry. She doesn't know I'm awake and her face is slack. She's not performing. I've noticed that she's started wearing my T-shirts, the oldest ones that have been washed so many times the cotton is thin, nearly transparent. "Sit me up," I tell her. "A., sit me up."

I mistook her for my mother yesterday. We couldn't get permission to have the IV at home, so I'm taking my morphine orally. I put eight purple pills, thirty milligrams each, on my tray, not knowing if I'd take them all and then, of course, taking them all. Sometime later Adrien brought in a basin of water and a bar of Ivory. I must have nodded out and when I woke up, she was washing the flats of my hands. You have had this done, we all have. When you were small you ate something sticky, watermelon or a Popsicle, and when you were finished, you were told to hold out your hands and somebody wiped at them, roughly, the wet napkin shredding as it rounded the skin between your fingers. "Enough, Ma," I said and tried to pull my hand away. Adrien grabbed my wrist and held on.

I'm a carpenter, a big man. Before I got sick, I could lift anything, move anything. Now I've got arms soft as a woman's. I'm not skinny the way cancer patients are supposed to be. In fact, I'm bloated from the steroids I forget why I'm taking.

This, believe it or not, isn't the most difficult period. Now, at least, we know who we are. I am the patient; Adrien is the nurse. The months after I was diagnosed but before I was so sick I had to stay in bed were the worst. People don't know about this time. We didn't. What happens is you're diagnosed in the hospital then sent home. You're an outpatient. You drive your car, have your same old arguments, meet other couples for dinner in Mexican restaurants. Except that in your most intimate and tender moments, neither of you knows what to say. The dividing line has been drawn. It's exhausting, keeping so much at bay. Bruised is how you feel. And you haven't gotten any morphine yet. Doctors and nurses encourage temperance in the terminally ill. You hurt all the time.

I came into the bedroom and found Adrien crying over a medical encyclopedia. She slammed it shut, looked up at me as if I'd caught her going through my wallet. I made her show me what she'd been looking at. Spread across two pages was a bar graph illustrating the five-year survival rates for various kinds of cancers. The column labeled "Metastatic Lung Cancer" was empty. I heaved the book in her direction, hoped to hit her, didn't, told her to get away from me, said I couldn't take any more of her fucking big-eyed sympathy. Her mouth quivered with rage. Her shout was throaty and raw. "I'd love to get away from you. That's what I want more than anything, to be away from you."

She said she needed something to relieve stress, to help her sleep at night. She started walking. It began reasonably enough, twenty minutes, a half hour, but soon she was doing ten and fifteen miles at a clip. She'd be gone all afternoon and into the evening. When she got home, she'd stand before me and announce: I just walked to Teaneck, to Paterson, to Ridge-wood, all towns miles and miles away. If she wasn't home by dark, I'd get in the car and go look for her. I rarely found her because she took crazy circuitous routes but when I did, she'd be striding along with her head down, fiddling with the dial on her Walkman.

We spent so much time at the hospital being sent all over hell. Here for a chest Xray, there for blood work, someplace else to fill out insurance forms or pick up prescriptions. We'd separate in the interest of efficiency, meet later at whatever place was easiest for me. Something started happening. As soon as we'd spot each other, we'd start waving and we'd keep doing it, eyes locked, smiling or not, until we were together again.

It was Adrien who told me I had cancer. I'd just been brought back to my room. My doctor had left for a conference in L.A. right after the bronchoscopy. He called from the airport. Adrien talked to him for not more than a minute, turned away from the phone, crossed her arms. Cells related to lung cancer. The tumor on my hip was secondary. The primary site was in my left bronchial tube.

She leaned over me and put four fingers on my cheek. I flattened myself against the mattress. She was coping already, monitoring my response so she could shape hers. As far as I was concerned, she had nothing to cope with. Her part was easy. Adrien as heroine was out of the question.

A nurse came in just then to take my temperature and I was glad. She had the spirited look of so many of the nurses at Memorial. They were forthright and sensible, worked twelve-hour shifts. The ones who kept their nails nice, who wore bright things in their hair, were easy to love. I felt strangely content in the company of nurses, women to whom all I'd ever been was dying.

Adrien picked up on my response to the pretty young nurses and rallied when I flirted with them. If she walked in to find me passing the time with one—they talked to me about their boyfriends, about living in New York for the first time—Adrien would smile indulgently. Go on and flirt. The nurse fiddled with the computerized thermometer and Adrien backed out of the room, said she had to put money in her parking meter.

She doesn't know that I watched her walk across First Avenue. She stepped out from under the awning, headed off in one direction then stopped and looked the other way, not remembering, I knew, where she'd parked the car. She'd come right from work, wore a black and white blazer that gleamed in the sun. As far as I could tell, she wasn't crying, which surprised me. I'd assumed she'd run off to cry. She looked ordinary, maybe slightly dazed. If you knew the way she usually charged around, you'd notice a difference but to a stranger she probably looked like a secretary on lunch, maybe a secretary whose boss had snapped at her unfairly before she left the office. She squeezed her bottom lip and looked into the faces of people who passed her.

When she came back, her eyes were red. She'd found someplace to cry, a ladies' room most likely. Adrien is a great bathroom cryer. She'll stand in front of the mirror and look right into her own eyes. The sight of herself crying keeps her crying.

THE last time I was hospitalized I got my first morphine. No more Tylenol or codeine. A shot in the IV, a rescue dose. It's nothing like novocaine. It didn't make me feel as if I no longer had a hip. The pain that had been the central fact of my existence for months backed the fuck off. It felt as if it were coming from inside layers of flannel. Winter pajamas warm from the dryer. Still with me but sound asleep.

A black woman in an aqua uniform brought me dinner. I found myself explaining to Adrien why it is people hate hospital food. What they give you is not that bad. It's just that eating in a hospital room is like having dinner in a public john. Urinals hooked to bed rails, gauze pads in the garbage cans, suction machines bubbling. I ate heartily while I talked, liking the dreamy feel of lukewarm food on my tongue, the sensation of my teeth meeting.

My uncle Jimmy came home from the war addicted to morphine. Once in a while he'd show up at our door and my mother would pull him inside. She'd go and see a woman she knew, somebody she'd worked with in the garment district. I'd sit on the front steps with Jimmy after he'd taken his shot. He'd talk about Normandy, about a soldier named Leonard. Sometimes it was Leonard who had saved Jimmy's life. Other times Jimmy had saved Leonard's. It was the same story to Jimmy. He thought he was telling one story. That's what morphine does, makes it not matter who saved whose life.

My father and my aunts would get furious with my mother for buying the dope. They'd lecture her about what was best for Jimmy and she wouldn't argue. She'd nod her head and avert her eyes and the next time Jimmy came around she'd put on her coat and go see her lady friend. Jimmy was my mother's youngest brother.

When Adrien and the woman from the hospice program were making arrangements to bring me home, renting the hospital bed, ordering oxygen, they had a big discussion about my pain medication. Adrien was told to keep a log, how much she gave me when, how I seemed, groggy, alert, how dilated were my pupils. The first afternoon at home, Adrien uncapped the bottle, said let's see now. Give those to me, I said. My pain, my morphine.

I watched Adrien dry off after her shower last night. Though she doesn't have time to walk these days, I can still see the effects. There's a sleek sort of oval between her hipbone and thigh. She ran her hand over it, liked it, turned sideways in the mirror to admire it.

She was never much good when I was sick before, minor ailments like the flu and once I broke my ankle. "So how do you feel? Better?" she'd ask. But my God has she risen to this challenge. Her touch tries so hard to soothe. When she washes my hair, she uses the lather as a lubricant to rub the cords in my neck. When she has to be gone for any period of time, when the hospice nurse or one of my sisters-in-law takes over, I get panicky missing her. She feels it too, I know, because when she comes in, she makes a beeline for me, adjusts my pillow, brushes the hair off my forehead, kisses me on the lips five or six times, fast kisses without much pucker.

This is a side of her I never knew existed. It makes me sorry we never had kids. Now I can imagine Adrien rocking a baby, nursing one even.

She wasn't with me when a doctor told me to tell my family six months. I called her from a pay phone on Sixty-eighth Street, cried, said I wouldn't be home for a while. There's a bar upstate, a dive where middle-aged bikers hang out. I wanted to go there and drink and not talk. I thought I could stand to be there. "No," she said. "You have to come home. If I don't see you, I'll go crazy. Please, please come home." So I did. She was waiting outside when I got there. We drove eighty, ninety, a hundred miles an hour on the turnpike. No relief or release, no nothing for me.

WE'VE never had so many visitors. They come to see me, of course. What's funny is that we handle company in precisely the way we always did. Adrien is ill at ease, much too nice, eager for them to gather their shit and go. I, on the other hand, am the perfect host. Friends and family pull their chairs close to my bed and lean in, smiling. They want to stay but then I nod out and Adrien scurries around lowering shades and most people get the hint.

I can still get a rise out of her. I asked her for a glass of carrot juice and she went right to work, chopping the carrots and feeding them to the juicer. I took a sip and told her it was full of pulp. "I strained it," she said. "Maybe so but I can't drink it like this." She looked at me for three seconds, whisked the glass away, strained it two more times, set it down in front of me. "It's still pulpy," I said. She grabbed the glass and dumped it in the sink. "You don't like carrot juice," she snapped, "so don't ever ask for it again. You can have orange or apple. Forget about carrot."

I waved at her. Hey, Adrien. Hey.


I DON'T know if she means to show off. Maybe it's just that I'm so sick and she's so healthy. She strides across the kitchen, carries three bags of groceries at once, sits down almost never. Adrien the superwoman, pass the morphine.

I'm restless at night. Adrien sleeps in a cot she borrowed and set up beside my bed. I wake her up a lot. "A.," I say, "A., are you awake?" "Mmmmmmmm," she'll say and roll over to face me, the outline of her hip fine and strong under the white sheet that looks blue in the moonlight. I slip pills into my mouth and talk, say whatever words work their way to the surface. She doesn't answer, looks right in my eyes. Then I let her fall back to sleep for a while, until I need to wake her up again, until I need to tell her Adrien, I'm scared.

# Jane Smiley

# A Thousand Acres

**Winner of the Pulitzer Prize for Fiction
and the
US National Book Critics' Circle Award**

Larry Cook's farm is the largest in Zebulon County, Iowa, and a tribute to his hard work and single-mindedness. Proud and possessive, his sudden decision to retire and hand over the farm to his three daughters, is disarmingly uncharacteristic. Ginny and Rose, the two eldest, are startled yet eager to accept, but Caroline, the youngest daughter, has misgivings. Immediately, her father cuts her out.

In *A Thousand Acres* Jane Smiley transposes the *King Lear* story to the modern day, and in so doing at once illuminates Shakespeare's original and subtly transforms it.

'A near-miraculous success'                          *Washington Post*

'Commanding, mythic, beautiful'                          *Boston Globe*

'Powerful, poignant, intimate and involving'          *New York Times*

'While Smiley has written beautifully about families in all of her preceding books, her latest effort is her best; a family portrait that is also a near-epic investigation into the broad landscape, the thousand dark acres, of the human heart. The book has all the stark brutality of a Shakespearean tragedy.'          *Washington Post*

flamingo

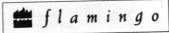 **flamingo**

Flamingo is a quality imprint publishing both fiction and non-fiction. Below are some recent titles.

## Fiction

- ☐ News From a Foreign Country Came *Alberto Manguel* £4.99
- ☐ The Kitchen God's Wife *Amy Tan* £4.99
- ☐ Moon Over Minneapolis *Fay Weldon* £5.99
- ☐ Isaac and His Devils *Fernanda Eberstadt* £5.99
- ☐ The Crown of Columbus *Michael Dorris & Louise Erdrich* £5.99
- ☐ A Thousand Acres *Jane Smiley* £5.99
- ☐ Dirty Weekend *Helen Zahavi* £4.50
- ☐ Mary Swann *Carol Shields* £4.99
- ☐ Cowboys and Indians *Joseph O'Connor* £5.99
- ☐ The Waiting Years *Fumiko Enchi* £5.99

## Non-fiction

- ☐ The Proving Grounds *Benedict Allen* £5.99
- ☐ The Quantum Self *Danah Zohar* £4.99
- ☐ Ford Madox Ford *Alan Judd* £6.99
- ☐ C. S. Lewis *A. N. Wilson* £5.99
- ☐ Into the Badlands *John Williams* £5.99
- ☐ Dame Edna Everage *John Lahr* £5.99
- ☐ Handel and His World *H. C. Robbins Landon* £5.99
- ☐ Taking It Like a Woman *Ann Oakley* £5.99

You can buy Flamingo paperbacks at your local bookshop or newsagent. Or you can order them from Fontana Paperbacks, Cash Sales Department, Box 29, Douglas, Isle of Man. Please send a cheque, postal or money order (not currency) worth the purchase price plus 24p per book (maximum postage required is £3.00 for orders within the UK).

NAME (Block letters)_____

ADDRESS_____

_____

_____